P9-CNC-230

WITHDRAWN

The
Truth About
Twinkie Pie

The
Truth About
Twinkie Pie

by Kat Yeh

Little, Brown and Company
New York Boston

This book is a work of fiction. Names, characters, places, and incidents are the product of the author's imagination or are used fictitiously. Any resemblance to actual events, locales, or persons, living or dead, is coincidental.

Copyright © 2015 by Kat Yeh

All rights reserved. In accordance with the U.S. Copyright Act of 1976, the scanning, uploading, and electronic sharing of any part of this book without the permission of the publisher is unlawful piracy and theft of the author's intellectual property. If you would like to use material from the book (other than for review purposes), prior written permission must be obtained by contacting the publisher at permissions@hbgusa.com. Thank you for your support of the author's rights.

Little, Brown and Company

Hachette Book Group
1290 Avenue of the Americas, New York, NY 10104
Visit us at lb-kids.com

Little, Brown and Company is a division of Hachette Book Group, Inc.
The Little, Brown name and logo are trademarks of Hachette Book Group, Inc.

The publisher is not responsible for websites (or their content) that are not owned by the publisher.

First Edition: January 2015

"This Is Just to Say" by William Carlos Williams, from THE COLLECTED POEMS: VOLUME I, 1909-1939, copyright © 1938 by New Directions Publishing Corp. Reprinted by permission of New Directions Publishing Corp.

Library of Congress Cataloging-in-Publication Data

Yeh, Kat.
The truth about Twinkie Pie / by Kat Yeh.—First edition.
pages cm
Summary: "When twelve-year-old GiGi and her big sister DiDi move to Long Island from South Carolina for GiGi to attend a fancy new private school, GiGi has a new recipe for success and makes new friends, but then discovers a family secret that turns her life upside-down"—Provided by publisher.
ISBN 978-0-316-23662-1 (hardcover)—ISBN 978-0-316-23671-3 (library ebook edition)—ISBN 978-0-316-23659-1 (ebook) [1. Moving, Household—Fiction. 2. Sisters—Fiction. 3. Mothers—Fiction.] I. Title.
PZ7.Y3658Tr 2015
[Fic]—dc23
2013042076

10 9 8 7 6 5 4 3 2 1

RRD-C

Printed in the United States of America

For Jaz
What you make is up to you.

ONE

Truth is, I knew the lady with the green scarf was not Mama. But I followed her anyway.

Mama's hair was supposed to be brown and wavy like mine. Or brown and curly like DiDi's. Not pale and blond and straight like rain. Also, Mama was dead. So yes. I knew the lady with the green scarf was likely not her, but I still followed along. Just for a bit. It was this game I play sometimes: What If.

What if it was all a big mistake and Mama didn't die the way I've always been told? What if she didn't want to leave me and DiDi, but had no choice? Like, maybe, she was working for the government on some top secret mission where her death had to be faked and her identity changed. After all,

Mama had been the best hairdresser in South Carolina, so she would know all about hair color and makeovers.

...But see, that doesn't really work out, because DiDi always says Mama was so popular, she had a line of people waiting on her at the beauty parlor from opening to closing, every day. Not leaving much time for government spying. So, unless the FBI was hunting down the masterminds behind all that sprayed-up hair at the Piggly Wiggly (which, in my humble opinion, would make a fine government priority), I guess Mama wouldn't be their first choice of spy.

Still, I couldn't help thinking...What If.

Now, following the lady with the green scarf during the Grand Opening of a brand-new Super Saver was not exactly what I thought I'd be doing my very first week as a resident of this fine town on Long Island, New York. But then our old neighbor, Davey Dylan, hadn't planned on that snapping turtle biting off his pinky finger five summers ago. It just happened. When he saw that turtle heading out to nap under a rotten log, it made him think of snapper soup. When I saw the lady with the green scarf heading for the cosmetics, it made me think of Mama.

As she slowed down near the lipsticks, my heart started beating really fast inside me. I watched as she looked up and down the aisle. Searching and searching.

She reached out her hand. I held my breath.

But then she grabbed hold of some nothing-brand lip gloss, and just like that, it was over. After all, Mama had been a Revlon lady all the way. And there were no What Ifs about it.

"May we help you?"

Two Super Saver clerks were standing behind me, looking all official with their big old name tags: KATE, ASST. MGR., and TIM, TRAINEE. Tim was also wearing this big button that said:

SUPER TRAINEE!
TELL ME IF I'M DOING A SUPER JOB!

Now, I was supposed to be looking for maraschino cherries, so DiDi could make Mama's Famous Twinkie Pie. But anytime I'm in a store and a clerk asks, "May I help you?" these words always come out before I can stop them:

"Do you have Revlon's Cherries in the Snow lipstick? In the Classic Gold Case, please?"

Asst. Mgr. Kate leaned way down and touched the tip of my nose with a pearly painted finger. "Listen to you with that little southern accent. You are adorable. And out here shopping all by yourself for lipstick. Is it for your mommy?"

Now, the worst part about looking like a ten-year-old when you're twelve is that no one takes you seriously and just answers your questions. Add freckles and a name like GiGi and grown-ups just about lose their minds thinking you're too cute for words. DiDi always says my being extra brainy trumps being tall any day and I should just look people in the eye and Say It Like It Is.

So I did.

"No, ma'am. My mama died when I was a baby."

Dead Mamas have a way of changing things.

"Oh. Dear. Let me find out for you, right away." And she got right down to business, talking into this headset thing she was wearing. Like she was part of the Lipstick Secret Service or something. I held perfectly still until she looked up and slowly shook her head. "I'm sorry, no. We don't carry that shade."

Now, I already knew Cherries in the Snow wasn't in that store. I knew it wasn't in any store, anywhere, in the whole country or planet, and hadn't been for a good while. So it's not like I was even hopeful or anything. That would be plain silliness. It's just ... there's something about asking for Impossible Things. For one little second, they feel Possible.

I smiled even though the disappointment pressed into me like a too-tight belt buckle. "Oh, that's okay. Thanks anyway. Could you tell me where I can find maraschino cherries, then? The red kind in a jar, please."

After Dead Mamas, maraschino cherries were probably like a vacation, because Asst. Mgr. Kate smiled as wide as the day. "For that, we'll turn to our newest trainee, Tim."

She gestured to Tim, who was standing there with his shirt tucked in a whole lot tighter than I'm guessing most shirts would want. He gave a nervous nod.

4

"As part of our Grand Opening Super Trainees Challenge, Tim will be back with any one of our quality Super Saver Products in under ninety seconds or it's yours free!" And just like that, she had a big old stopwatch in her hand. "Maraschino cherries!" she called out. "Red—in jar—go!"

Click! Tick, tick, tick, tick, tick . . .

And off he went. Looking like he was going to fetch those cherries if he had to tackle his own granny to get to the last jar.

I looked at Asst. Mgr. Kate.

She looked at me.

Tick, tick, tick, tick, tick . . .

And that stopwatch, it kept right on counting down the seconds like the whole place would explode or something if Tim failed to come back in time. People always come up with these ideas that they think are all fun and games, but truth is they're just plain stressful.

Like DiDi's favorite cooking show on TV—the one where the contestants get this Basket of Mystery Ingredients. And whatever is in there, they have to cook. I swear once they pulled out chicken feet and pancake mix. Then, just like that, the clock went off and they had to make a gourmet dinner. During the last ten seconds, the judges always start wringing their hands like the world's going to end, practically crying, "Get the food on the plate! Just get the food on the plate!" DiDi loves this show. But I don't.

It's just not fair.

If you don't get to pick your own ingredients and take your own sweet time, how do you even have a chance to make something worthwhile?

Tick, tick, tick, tick, tick...

And what do you know. There he was. Speed-walking around the corner. Big button shining. Shirt tucked in tight as ever. Holding up that jar of cherries like it was a chicken feet and pancake soufflé.

Click.

Tim handed me the jar and snapped right back to standing at attention.

"Is there anything else we can get for you, young lady?" Asst. Mgr. Kate began to raise that stopwatch again.

"Oh, no thank you," I said, and started to walk away. But then I remembered something and turned back to Tim. "You're doing a Super Job."

That Tim, Trainee. His face split into a grin that was half triumph and half relief, and without missing a beat, he gave me the old wink and double gun fingers and said, "Thank you, miss—and *you* have a Super Day!"

Asst. Mgr. Kate couldn't have looked prouder.

If my life were a TV cooking show, it's no mystery what I'd want in my Basket of Ingredients. But, like I said before, you don't get to pick. No one does. And besides, even if I could, I don't think there's a basket out there big and magic enough to hold Mama and her lipstick.

two

The first thing DiDi did when I handed her the maraschino cherries was hold them way up high and sashay across our kitchen calling out, "Sweet Stuff coming through!" Then she peeked back over her shoulder and did a little bam-bam with her hips. "And I'm not talkin' about the maraschino cherries."

DiDi is always cracking jokes like that. Like at dinner last night, she yelled out, "Hot Stuff coming through!" Big wink. "And I'm not talkin' about the tuna noodle casserole."

Of course, she didn't think it was all that funny last Thanksgiving when she was sweating under that heavy platter and I yelled, "Big Turkey coming through! And I'm not talkin' about Thanksgiving dinner."

DiDi set the cherries down on the counter and got right

to work making Mama's Famous Twinkie Pie. We usually only have Twinkie Pie once a year for our birthdays, which are exactly nine years, nine days, and nine hours apart. But today, DiDi made an exception because she wanted to bring it to Welcome Night at my new school, where all the parents would get to meet the teachers and stuff. It was hosted by this committee that I guess controls the universe, seeing how much DiDi wanted to impress them.

Whenever DiDi makes Mama's recipes, she likes to pretend she's starring in her own TV cooking show. Sometimes she even puts on a nice shirt for the occasion. I told her she should let her curls go all loose and pretty, which would look great on camera, but I don't think there's been a day in her life she didn't have them pulled back in a tight little knot.

I got myself nice and comfy. My job is to watch and DiDi's is to ignore any suggestions I might make.

"Now remember, GiGi," she said in her cooking show voice. "The secret to Twinkie Pie is to make it just like Mama did, and that means using maraschino cherries so you can make your whipped topping the perfect shade of pinky-red. Just like—"

I said the next part with her: "Cherries in the Snow!"

Ever since I was a little bitty thing, whenever DiDi made Twinkie Pie, she'd tell me the story of Mama and Revlon's Cherries in the Snow lipstick.

"Cherries in the Snow was Mama's favorite lipstick and

the only one she'd ever wear. Why, if she walked into a drug-store and they were out of it, she'd walk right out that door and down the street to the next store and the next and the next until she found it."

I remember how happy it made me to imagine my mama being so particular about her lipstick. I imagined she looked just like DiDi with her tilty nose and curvy top lip. I'd pretend the little pink candles DiDi put on top of the Twinkie Pie were tiny lipsticks, pulling them off and spreading the frosting on my own mouth. "I wish I had Cherries an' Snow...." I used to say.

"I wish you did, too, baby girl," she'd answer. "But no one does anymore. The good people at Revlon haven't made that lipstick in about a hundred years."

Of course, I found out later it was nowhere near a hundred years, but it didn't matter either way. It was gone. When she lit the candles, DiDi would lean in close and say, "Make a wish, G. Only... well, you don't want to go wasting a perfectly good birthday wish on—" Then she'd put her cheek next to mine and whisper, "Why don't I just make one for the both of us?"

And we'd blow out the candles together. Even as a little girl, I knew what she was worried about. Me wishing for things that would never come true. That would never come back.

I watched as DiDi set out all her bowls and mixing spoons in a nice tidy row. She winked up at her imaginary camera.

"Now, I always like to make the pudding ahead of time, so it's nice and chilled when I'm ready to get started."

I was sitting on one of our new twirly bar stools. They slid under this counter that's like a big window between the kitchen and the living room, so you can pass food out to the people sitting there like you're at the diner. Before we moved, our friend Lori found the stools in the Dumpster behind this bar she used to go to. She was pretty handy now that she was on the wagon, and she gave them nice new seat covers. Except for some scratches on the legs, they were perfectly fine.

"Did I tell you the thing Lori said when she called?" I twirled a little bit right. Then left. And then right again.

DiDi's behind was sticking out of the fridge, where she was looking for the pudding. "What's that, baby girl?"

"It's no biggie...but, well, you know that salesman she dated?"

"Lori dated lots of salesmen, honey."

"The No-Good Lying Son of a Walnut who was married with like ten kids."

"Oh. Him. Go on."

"Well..." I paused for a second. "He calls on all the big drugstores, and he told her that makeup companies sometimes bring back old colors—the really special ones, anyway." I peeked over at her to see what she would say.

DiDi had set the pudding on the counter and was now

unwrapping Twinkies and slicing them up. "Now, there are a lot of Twinkie pies out there in the world, but Mama's is the only one that's double-decker. Isn't that right, G?"

"Uh...yes. I guess."

"After you have your crust and your Twinkies all set up, go on and get your maraschino cherries." DiDi looked up and snapped her fingers at me. "Earth to G. Pass the cherries, please."

"What? Oh." I looked over at the jar of cherries, but instead of reaching for them, I got up and went to a Super Saver bag I'd left by the sofa. I held it out to her.

"What's that?"

I poured it out on the counter. A jumble of ruby-red cherries tumbled out, fresh and shiny, rolling all over DiDi's neat work space. "They had them at the Super Saver. I wanted to surprise you—I thought maybe—"

DiDi put a hand out to stop them. "The recipe says maraschino cherries, G."

"Maybe you could use both—or maybe you could just put these on top or—"

DiDi quickly gathered the cherries together and put them back in the bag. She rolled the top down nice and tight. "Why don't you stick these in the fridge? You can have them for a snack later."

I nodded and took the bag.

"I can see you pouting from here, G. Don't you like having Mama's recipes the way she made them? To remember her?" One curl slipped out of her bun. She reached up and tucked it back in.

"I know, D, it's just that you never—Nothing."

I put the bag away, handed her the maraschino cherries, and sat back down.

DiDi watched me for a second, then sighed and got back to work. I twirled a few more times, then reached out toward Mama's Cookbook and gently ran my fingers over it.

"Can I?"

DiDi paused in the middle of fussing with her cherries. "Okay, G, just please—"

"I know, I know. I'll be careful. I promise."

On the outside, Mama's Cookbook is just a regular old three-ring binder like you have at school. But inside are Mama's recipes, all nice and typed up or handwritten with little cutout pictures and notes and such. You can tell exactly what Mama was like by looking through it. She didn't do anything unless she thought it was special and fun and one of a kind with some sort of little twist. I think she would've wanted DiDi to change things up every once in a while, but that wasn't happening anytime soon. DiDi could move us 800 miles. But she couldn't put fresh cherries into Twinkie Pie.

I turned the pages carefully, making sure I didn't bend or wrinkle anything. Mama's Cookbook is like the fancy room in a house where I'm only allowed to go if I promise not to touch any of the fussy throw pillows. It's the only thing of Mama's that DiDi and I have. And it was plain dumb luck that our babysitter, Miss Linda, asked DiDi to bring it to her place that night when she was watching me. The night of the fire, I mean. I was only a little baby, so I don't even remember any of it. DiDi tells me the worst part was that it took everything. We don't even have a photo of Mama. Sometimes I squeeze my eyes shut and try to see if I can picture her face. But it never works. DiDi says I don't need a dumb old photo. Every time we make her food, it's our way of remembering the way she was.

I only ever asked once about having a daddy, and DiDi said, "Best forget about him, GiGi. Everything you got in the brain department you got from Mama. She may have been a hairdresser, but she was brainy like you and had big plans." I liked that.

After a while, I peeked out. DiDi was finishing up the pie, but her yakky cooking show voice was gone.

You don't exactly have to be a government agent to figure out that DiDi is super-sensitive about people messing with Mama's recipes. Adding fresh cherries to Twinkie Pie is practically the same as suggesting she throw in a sardine or two. I don't even know why she watches that Mystery Basket show, seeing how much she hates surprise ingredients. Surprises of any kind, really.

Except for maybe when we won that one million dollars last spring.

Of course, DiDi says she wasn't surprised at all. She had planned on winning. We don't talk about it to anyone. But if we did, I guess most people would be wondering what millionaires living on the North Shore of Long Island are doing in a one-bedroom apartment above the salon where DiDi cuts hair. Going about life like we were still in that trailer park back in South Carolina.

My Famous Twinkie Pie

- 3 cups vanilla wafer cookies, crushed to make 2 cups of coarse crumbs, plus 6 cookies crushed and set aside for garnish
- 6 tablespoons butter, melted
- ¼ teaspoon salt
- ¼ cup instant vanilla pudding mix (about half a box)
- 1 cup cold milk
- 2 cups heavy cream (divided into ½ cup and 1½ cups)
- 7 Twinkies
- 2 bananas, sliced
- 10-ounce jar of red maraschino cherries, drained and stemmed (save 2 tablespoons of juice and set one cherry aside for garnish)

You'll need a 9-inch springform pan.

Preheat your oven to 350°F. For the crust, mix the 2 cups of cookie crumbs with the melted butter and salt. Press it into the bottom of your springform pan. Put it in the oven for 12 minutes until it's golden brown. Take out the pan and let it cool. Meanwhile, make your pudding. Whisk the

15

pudding mix with the cold milk for 2 minutes until it thickens. In a separate bowl, beat the ½ cup of heavy cream until stiff peaks form (about 2 minutes on an electric hand mixer). Fold the whipped cream into the pudding mixture, and put it in the fridge for now.

Go on and find your favorite knife, and slice those Twinkies in half so they look like little thumbs. Line them, thumbs up, all around your pan in a circle on top of the crust. Then—you guessed it—arrange the banana slices in a nice layer. Then pour the pudding over everything.

Here's my special touch: Put the cherries in the blender—except for one cherry for the top of your pie! Add the 2 tablespoons of cherry juice, and just zap them up into cherry puree. In a fresh bowl, whip the remaining 1½ cups of heavy cream into stiff peaks. Then fold in your cherry puree until it's the perfect shade of pinky-red—just like Cherries in the Snow lipstick. (Now, I know you swear by your Love That Red, Mary Elizabeth, but don't you dare cross out my Cherries in the Snow and fill that in! There. I've said it plain and clear for anyone to see in case you do have the nerve to put your chicken scratch in here next time you borrow this.)

Anyway, pour your pinky-red topping over the pie and smooth it out. Garnish with the remaining crushed cookies. Top with one cherry.

Refrigerate till firm. Enjoy!

Serves 8–10.

three

The next day, while DiDi went to Welcome Night at Hill on the Harbor Preparatory (the best private school in the universe), I spent the evening sitting on the sofa, studying.

When I heard a *creeeeak!* out in our hallway, I looked up from my book. There are two apartments above the salon where we live. Ours and Kenneth's. He's our landlord, and our doors face each other in the little hallway at the top of the stairs. There's a sign on the front of our building that says it's Historical (which is just a fancy word for old). That means the doors have brass knobs and the ceilings have curly molding and if you step on the top step wrong, it gives a big old *creeeeak!* On the bright side, I told DiDi it was a built-in Burglar Alarm. She answered, "Too bad we don't have a built-in Kenneth Alarm, too."

Now, poor Kenneth wouldn't hurt a fly, but the second that stair creaks, he comes scrambling out of his apartment. Then just stands there, fidgeting and blushing and trying to figure out a way to say hi to DiDi. I'll just say it straight. DiDi is what people call a Real Beauty. I'll just mention that those same people call me a Real Brain and leave it at that.

The door opened a crack and DiDi came backing in.

"Well, this has sure been fascinating, Kenneth. But I got GiGi here and she needs help with her homework." Which is the biggest laugh ever, seeing as DiDi only finished up to eighth grade.

She slipped inside and shut the door behind her, shaking her head. "That man needs to loosen up, and I don't just mean that sad old ponytail of his." She was still holding the Twinkie Pie. It hadn't even been touched.

"What happen—I mean, hey, Double D..." I kind of waved.

"Hey, Double G." She went straight into the kitchen. "Saving the pie for later. There was already so much food, I guess it just got—shoved to the side."

I watched her put it in the fridge and start pacing around. I could see she had her Planning Hat on. DiDi gets like that whenever she wants to make some big pronouncement about

19

my future. "Did you study? Caught up and ready to go? You know how important this is."

"Yes, DiDi. I know, I know."

Our conversations always go something like that. I mentioned how DiDi called me brainy. Well, truth is I've never gotten a grade below an A+. Or a paper lower than a 100. DiDi says it's because I do everything 150%. She calls it my Recipe for Success. Now that I was about to start in this fancy new private school (which the brochure informed us was fondly referred to as Hill Prep by everyone), she said I'd have to work even harder. I had all the ingredients already. I just had to follow the recipe. Which is why I was studying before school even started.

DiDi kept pacing back and forth. I just waited.

"Double G," she said finally. "You know that big fancy party the school's having in November?"

"Sure," I said. "The weekend right before our birthdays—hang on!" I shuffled through a little pile of brochures on the table by the sofa. "Here it is—the Founder's Day Gala. In celebration of the day the school was 'founded.' Why can't they just say 'found'? It sounds funny."

She stopped pacing. "I don't know, G, but I can tell you what *I* found."

"What?"

DiDi put a hand on her hip. "I found myself a position as the head of the Refreshment Committee for that Gala."

"Get out!" I said, which is what I always say when she tells me something too good for words.

DiDi grinned. "If you let me back in." Which is how she always replies.

"Can I—would you let me help?" I asked. I just knew if DiDi made Mama's beautiful recipes, everyone would love them.

"Really? You want to?" DiDi looked pretty emotional for such a small thing.

I nodded. "We can make it like our own personal Birthday Gala!"

"I'd love that, G. I'd really love that. But we'll do it right this time. We'll make sure we really do it right, okay?"

She didn't have to worry about me. I'd keep my ideas to myself and let her do everything the exact way she wanted. DiDi never lets me on the camera side of the cooking show, but if she'd let me be her assistant just once, that was worth keeping my trap shut. "It's a deal, then." I held out my hand and we shook. "You and I are partners! We'll make it the best Gala ever! What should we put on the menu? Were they excited you wanted to do it?"

"Oh..." DiDi paused and bit her thumbnail. "Well, they were a little—You know, who cares? There's plenty of time to figure out all the details." She looked me right in the eyes. "GiGi, I think we'll love it here. We can decorate the apartment real nice. The school's so close, you can walk. Just think of all the money we'll save on gas. It just feels like the right time for the right change in our lives."

"I know it, DiDi."

That's when I realized it was also the right time to finally bring up something I'd been wanting to talk about since we got here. I cleared my throat. "D?" I said. "I wanted to discuss something with you that's super-important."

DiDi nodded, still in her planning place.

"I think—I mean, I have decided that—I want to change my name for the new school."

DiDi snapped out of her blank stare. "Change your name? Why? When? Where? How?"

I sighed. DiDi always gets like this when she panics. I call it Getting Grammatical. "Easy, DiDi. It's no big deal."

She started pacing again. "No big deal? Since when is changing your name no big deal?" She stopped and narrowed her eyes. "This isn't about those idiot boys still, is it?"

Back in third grade, these boys in my class, Jakey Renssler and Joey Feldman, overheard DiDi and me calling each other Double D and Double G, and they told everyone that we were named after bra sizes. I was so mad, I called them darn liars and marched right into the neighborhood JCPenney that afternoon after school and snuck into the ladies' underwear department. Well, not only did I find out that we *were* named after bra sizes—we were GINORMOUS bra sizes. Everyone called us The Bra Sisters for the next three years. And seeing as how it doesn't look like I'll be needing any kind of bra anytime soon, there was no way I was starting the new school on that foot. As DiDi would say, gossip's got legs.

I searched around for a way to explain. I'd thought about it long and hard. When you have a big old strange name like mine—which I never say out loud—it's hard to come up with pretty little nicknames. And seeing as DiDi and Lori were the ones who started calling me GiGi, I never even had a say in the matter. But after playing around with it in my head, I'd come up with a pretty good fit.

"You said it was the 'right time for the right change,' D—all I want is a new nickname. You have to admit my real name is the single most embarrassing name in human history. I know Mama had her reasons for picking it, but..."

No response. DiDi just sat there looking hurt.

I took a big breath and plunged ahead. "Well, I was thinking: What about... Leia?"

DiDi shook her head. "I don't like it."

My face started to run away from me, but I caught it. "Give it a chance, DiDi."

"Lay-ya? Like that snotty princess with the big hairy earmuffs from that old space movie?"

"DiDi, stop it. I'm serious. Please."

She threw her arms up. "Okay, fine. But there is no way

I'm going to remember, G—see? It's only been three seconds and already I don't know who you are. How are you going to do it?"

I didn't answer.

I figured it wasn't exactly the right time to tell her that changing my name was only the beginning.

four

Lately, I'd been thinking about Mama's Wish Pie an awful lot. Wish Pie is a kind of pie that sits around hoping no one notices it's Not Pecan Pie. Which doesn't even matter, because most people take one look and say, "That sure is a nice-looking pecan pie." Because it looks and smells and even tastes like pecan pie. People are always begging DiDi to tell them Mama's secret. But it's no big deal. That's the secret: acting like it's No Big Deal. I mean, if you're trying to be pecan pie, you don't go around shouting, "I'm Pecan Pie! I'm Pecan Pie!" You just look those pie judges in the face and act like it.

DiDi's Recipe for Success for me is pretty strict:

- I study.
- I do extra-credit work.

- I study.
- Oh, and did I mention I study?

She never even lets me do stuff like hang out with her at the salon. I mean, of course she gives me a new haircut like you're supposed to get for school. But she's never once even asked me what I want. It's always the same. Every time. No bangs. ("Why would you want hair in your eyes with all the studying you have to do?") No little feathers or curlicues. ("Honestly, G, you don't have time to fuss, with all your schoolwork.")

She just gives a wave of her hand and says, "I don't have all day to talk about it, G. Let me just give you the DiDi Special and get you back to your books." Then she cuts it into something nice and practical and easy to put in a ponytail.

I always think it might be nice to hang out and look at silly magazines with her, talk and chew gum, and sweep hair into big ugly piles, but if I have a second of free time, DiDi makes me do stuff like volunteer at the library. And I can tell you that hanging out in a building where you're not allowed to talk is not the best way to make friends.

So I decided to make myself a new Recipe for Success.

For how to be the new me, in my new school, in our new life.

- Choose my own darn name (one that's pretty and does not remind everyone of a ginormous bra size).
- Hang out with real friends my own age and not just grown-ups who think I'm adorable.
- Actually eat lunch in a real live school cafeteria at a real live table with real live seventh graders, instead of studying in the library To Advance My Educational Position.
- Be the girl Mama would be if she were here. Friendly. Funny. Confident. (Also, throwing in a zinger or two is always good.)
- In other words, do everything and anything to be the girl I never had a chance to be before.

DiDi says Wish Pie should have been named Stop All Your Bellyaching and Just Be Who You Are Pie. When I told her that was the dumbest name I'd ever heard, she said, "People don't care what you name it, G. They like pie for what's on the inside."

Either way, this time it was my recipe and I was going to be whatever kind of pie I wanted.

Wish Pie

- 1 cup packed light brown sugar
- 1 cup dark (it has to be dark!) corn syrup
- 2 tablespoons butter, melted
- A pinch of salt
- 3 eggs
- ⅔ cup old-fashioned rolled oats
- 1 teaspoon vanilla
- ⅔ cup sweetened shredded coconut
- A ready-made graham cracker pie shell

Preheat your oven to 375°F. Mix the sugar, syrup, butter, and salt in a saucepan. Easy, easy cook over medium heat, stirring just till the sugar dissolves. Remove the pan from the heat and let it rest somewhere safe and peaceful.

Beat your eggs until foamy in a separate bowl. Now, you're going to want to let that syrup mixture cool a bit before you add the eggs or you'll end up with scrambled egg pie, and I can't picture too many people wishing for that! Once the syrup has cooled, blend in the eggs, mix well, and then stir in the oats, vanilla, and coconut. Pour into the pie shell.

Bake at 375°F for 45 minutes, till it's not too dark. And not too light. Just the perfect golden brown. (Give it a peek at 35 minutes because your oven may run a little hotter and you don't want the crust to burn.)

Now, y'all stop sitting around wishing you were something you're not and just get on out there and Be!

Serves 8.

five

I had my new name.

I had my locker combination memorized.

I had new paper and new pencils and a new eraser that smelled just like new erasers are supposed to.

But best of all, I had a brand-new uniform with a gray skirt and white shirt with a little tie thingie, and a nice navy blazer. For the first time ever, I had things that had never been passed down from anyone or bought on sale at the church thrift. It made me think that this new private school just might have something to it.

Now, DiDi almost got killed getting me into my old school, so I'm not sure why she wanted me to leave it. I'm dead serious. My old school was in a different town pretty far away from where we lived, but every year, they'd let fifty students send in applications from outside the district—first come, first served. When the date came up, DiDi borrowed a tent and spent the night on the District Office steps in the pouring rain with thunder and lightning. In the middle of the night, a tree across the way was hit and brought down a telephone pole. But DiDi wouldn't budge. The next day, she was the first one in. Crazy, if you ask me. I'd get top grades no matter where I went, but DiDi said it was the best school in South Carolina. She didn't care that she had to haul me back and forth, forty-five minutes each way, twice a day. She was over the moon about that school.

Well, now she was over the moon about Hill Prep, with its advanced classes and fancy teachers. Yakkity, yakkity, yak. But I didn't care about any of those things. I took one look at my new uniform and knew I'd never have to wear the sad old things DiDi used to send me to school in. Looking like a ratty tomboy. A ratty tomboy who hid in the library every day behind a pile of books, that is. Not quite belonging with the rough kids. Not quite belonging with the fancy ones, either. Not really belonging anywhere.

But those days were gone.

For the first time, I would look just like everyone else.

And maybe, just maybe, that meant I would look like someone's friend.

Now, I had gotten the school map the week before and traced paths to all my classes so I'd never be late for any of them. It had this big old-fashioned-looking crest with the school name stamped on it, and when I first stepped on that campus, I understood why. Those big grand buildings looked like they would be positively offended if you didn't put a crest on them. My old school was big, too, but it was more like a big fat square.

The buildings at Hill Prep had balconies and chimneys and wavy-glass windows. Pretty gardens and hedges and benches scattered everywhere just in case someone might want to stop in their tracks and relax. I read that the whole thing used to be some big old estate that some big old rich guy decided to make into some big old school.

A few years ago, they needed to expand the middle school, so they added this section. The kids named it The Honeycomb. The center was shaped like an octagon with a ceiling that reached two stories high. The first floor was completely lined with stacked cubbies and lockers, all pale golden wood and shining like little beehives. The top floor was classrooms, with a big center balcony so you could look all the way down. And the whole thing was filled with windows. I peeked around while I put my books in my locker and saw that a lot of the kids had theirs decorated with paper and notes stuck on them.

Welcome back!

I missed yoooooo!

How was your summer?

Scribbled hearts and smiley faces and stickers everywhere. I felt a little bad that I didn't even know anyone to give a note to. Or get one from. But that was going to change.

Because along with my new uniform, I had my new Recipe for Success, and today it was telling me to march right across that Honeycomb with my chin way up, all fast and confident and, most importantly, looking like I was in a rush and that was the reason why I wasn't talking to all those hundreds of people I didn't know.

Now, I'm good at math, but I must have miscalculated my chin angle, because three seconds into that Honeycomb and—*bam!*—I slammed into some kind of force field and landed sprawled out on the floor.

"Sorry! Sorry, are you okay?" I heard the force field say.

I guess I got hit pretty hard, because when I opened my eyes, I forgot how to talk. All I could think about was how I never liked it when people used the word *beautiful* to describe a boy. Even if he was. Like at DiDi's old salon, she used to work with this man she always referred to as Harley, My Beautiful Gay Best Friend.

"Uh, hello...are you okay?"

See, I think when you describe people, you can't just say stuff like Beautiful or Ugly. You need to get down to the truth of it. For example: Jakey Renssler had a Face Like Yesterday's Dog Food and that Joey Feldman? Dumb as a Bag of Underwear.

"...should I call the nurse?"

That snapped me out of it. "Huh?"

"Hi...are you okay?" The force field looked a little worried. Like maybe he was wondering about the side effects of a blow to the head.

Was I staring? I tried to get up and slipped. "Ow—I mean, uh, hi, I'm G—"

Darn it.

"G?"

I made this noise. DiDi calls it a guffaw. It sort of sounds like you're choking on your own snot but enjoying the heck out of it. I tried to follow it with a little laugh, but that came out mostly guffaw, too. "Oh no—not G. It's—I'm Leia. Leia Barnes. Hi." I held out a hand.

The force field took my hand and shook it. "I'm Trip."

I liked how his tie was kind of loose and rumpled...and how his hair kept falling into his face. He pushed it back. Brown eyes. Not too dark. Not too light. Just perfect. Like Wish Pie.

"Huh?"

"Trip."

"Oh no, I didn't trip. I think you knocked into me—"

"No—my name is Trip. I'm really sorry, I was going to English and you kind of came out of nowhere...."

"English? Me too. First period. Mr. McGuire. Room 18."

34

He looked down at my hand, which was still gripping his. Then smiled and pulled me up. "Well, you're going the wrong way."

And that's how I ended up walking to my first class on my first day of school, side by side with this—this—okay, fine—this Beautiful Boy. Along the way, Trip stopped every few steps. Waved to people. Introduced me around. Talked to practically every single person in existence. Laughing and saying things like "Okay, okay, I *tripped* the new girl." Everyone seemed to want to smile at me just because I was with him. They'd hear the story and then pass it on.

Pretty soon, all these kids were yelling out things like "Hey, New Girl! Don't trip!" But I didn't mind, because it was all good-natured.

See, gossip can go either way. It can be friendly and fun like with Trip. Or it can be like those mean stories we used to hear back in South Carolina about Dead Drunk Donna. They said she was this crazy old lady who took all her gold and melted it down to make a box of golden bullets. Then she sat outside, waiting and waiting. Till finally one night, when she was Dead Drunk, she shot a bear. Left it tied to a tree to scare everyone off.

When we arrived on the second floor, where our classroom was, I stopped and looked over the balcony. Down to that place in the middle of The Honeycomb where, with one fateful fall, I'd left the old me behind. I didn't have to walk into that classroom as boring old freckle-faced GiGi from South Carolina, because there was a new girl in town now.

The Girl Who Tripped Over Trip.

I was practically famous.

And I didn't need golden bullets or a dead bear tied to a tree.

All I had to do was trip over a Beautiful Boy.

Love at First Salad

Better watch out, now! Some things are just so beautiful, all it takes is one look and you'll feel like you're falling in love.

- A 21-ounce can of cherry pie filling
- A 20-ounce can of crushed pineapple, drained
- A 7-ounce bag of sweetened flaked coconut
- A 14-ounce can of sweetened condensed milk
- A 16-ounce container of whipped topping
- 2 cups mini-marshmallows
- 1 cup pecans, plus more for garnish
- A small head of curly leaf lettuce

Mix all your ingredients except for the lettuce in a large bowl in the order they're listed. Then pour it into a 9-by-13-inch baking pan and freeze overnight.

When you're all ready to serve, line little glass bowls with leaves of curly lettuce, to make a pretty cup for each guest. Then put a nice fat scoop of your frozen salad on top. You can put a couple of pecans on top, too.

Now, I've seen a lot of beautiful salads in my day, but the best thing about this one is that not only is it beautiful, but it's also sweet as can be. Through and through. And if you ask me, that's what makes it everyone's favorite.

Serves 10-12.

SIX

I've always been what you might call a Front Row type of girl, but Trip led me all the way to the back. I slipped into the seat next to him, smiling. I couldn't believe it. My Recipe for Success was already working. I was Leia. New Girl. Sitting in the back row next to a boy with Wish Pie eyes and floppy hair who was friends with the whole school.

And then it happened.

"Well, now. I think roll call is going to start with a big bang. Are you present, Miss—Galileo Galilei Barnes?" Mr. McGuire looked up from his sheet.

There it was. My full name in all its embarrassing glory.

For a brainy person, I can be pretty dumb. I had completely forgotten about roll call. I halfway raised my hand.

"Um ... here," I said.

Trip looked at me and mouthed, "Galileo?"

Mr. McGuire leaned back on his desk. "I think we may have to interrupt this important roll call to bring you a message from our sponsor. Does this name have some kind of special significance or story you'd like to tell us about, Miss Barnes?"

I glanced at Trip and took a deep breath. I wasn't used to being around people who didn't know about Mama and my name and me. But like I said, DiDi has this thing about Saying It Like It Is.

So I did.

"Well, my mama was a hairdresser, but she had this big dream that what she really wanted to be one day was a—an astronomer. You know, like, the kind of scientist who studies the stars." There were a few giggles in the classroom, which Mr. McGuire hushed right away. "And when I was born, she saw I had this birthmark." I pointed to the little white star on my forehead. "So she named me Galileo Galilei after this, um, scientist guy who I guess was really into studying stars and stuff...." I didn't want Mr. McGuire to think I was dumb on my very first day. I had all As in science; it's just that I'd always been so mad that Mama couldn't find an astronomer named Kaylee or Alyssa that I never wanted to read up on that Galileo. As I waited for Mr. McGuire to say something, I added, "But everyone calls me G—"

Darn it.

40

"G?"

"I—I mean Leia."

Mr. McGuire looked pleased, like maybe he had made a scientific discovery himself. "Well, thank you, Miss Barnes, for your charming and articulate introduction." He gave me a nod. "There's a club you should look for when the Club and Activities Fair rolls around. You'll know it when you see it— and let me know if you want to borrow some books on that Galileo guy. He did a lot more than study 'stars and stuff.'" He went back to his list. "James Benton?"

Trip was studying my face like there was going to be a quiz on me later.

"What?" I whispered.

"Nothing—just..." He pushed the hair out of his eyes and looked at me again. "I—I liked your story." Then he smiled. "Cool name, G-Girl."

Before I could stop myself, I was smiling back from one side of my head to the other. Then I remembered my new Recipe for Success. Always have a little zinger ready. "Yeah, but not as cool as being named after what happens when your big toe meets a crack in the sidewalk."

The boy sitting in front of us turned to give me a high five. "Hah! Sorry, bro—but you *are* named after an accident."

"Shut up, Fender," Trip said, but he was laughing.

"Mr. Billy Fender, is there anything you'd like to share with the class?" Mr. McGuire called out.

"No, sir," the boy answered. "Just extending salutations to the new girl who tackled my best bud this morning."

"Ah! Well, in light of your always-impressive vocabulary, Mr. Fender, I will allow this small disruption." He tipped an imaginary hat to the boy, who tipped one back.

Trip shook his head, smiling, then peeked over at me a couple of times. As he leaned back into his seat, the girl who was sitting on the other side of him suddenly came into view. She had the longest, prettiest hair I'd ever seen in my life. It fell straight down to her waist like a dark curtain.

Perfectly matching her dark eyes, which were glaring right into mine.

I kind of mentioned before about how DiDi is a stickler when it comes to messing around with Mama's recipes. Well, there is this thing I do that makes her all-out crazy. I will sneak the Love at First Salad out of the freezer before it has sat overnight, which DiDi swears is the key to making it perfect. But it's because I like to pick out the pecans. I do this thing where I plug up my ears with my fingers so I can hear the sound of them echoing around in my head while I munch away. Whenever DiDi opens the freezer and finds her salad with little holes poked into it, she shoots me eyes like daggers.

Well, this girl next to Trip?

The look she was shooting me put DiDi's to shame.

SEVEN

Where did you get the name Trip?"

We had been in every class together that morning, and now we were walking toward the cafeteria for lunch. I didn't catch Trip's real name during roll call, but it had sounded like Something-Something Hedgeclipper the Fourteenth. I always thought nicknames were interesting. Like, GiGi obviously stands for the *G*s in *Galileo Galilei*. And I knew this boy back home whose real name was Buford Ballsy, only everyone called him The Butt on account of how he loved nothing better than to moon you from the school bus window. Though if you ask me, it's a pretty sad situation if your real name is worse than being called The Butt.

"Did you used to trip a lot as a kid or something?"

"No, it's short for"—he made a face—"Triple. Because I'm the third. Bradford Breckinridge Davis the Third. Lame, right?"

"Oh no, I really like it. You're just like Thurston Howell the Third."

"Is he new here?"

"No, he was the rich guy from that old TV show about the boat that broke down on a desert island—you know the one?"

"No."

"Well, it was about a whole bunch of people that get ship-wrecked, and there's a professor who's, like, the smartest man in the universe and a movie star and some farm girl who was always in short-shorts. Anyway, Thurston Howell the Third was the millionaire."

"What happens?"

"I never actually watched it, but my sister, DiDi, used to tell me about it, because it was our mama's favorite show growing up." I smiled. "DiDi says Mama was a real feminist. Like, completely ahead of her time. When she was little, she thought it wasn't fair that Thurston Howell got to be a Third but she didn't know any girls who were. So she decided right there and then to start a tradition that every firstborn girl in the family should be named Delta Dawn, like her, till there was a Third. So my big sister is Delta Dawn the Second."

Trip looked at me. "Delta Dawn?"

"It was this really famous country song the year Mama

was born," I said. It's funny how names work out. Here DiDi and Mama were named after an old country song, and they were both hairdressers. And I was named after one of the most famous scientists of all time, and, well, I doubted I would ever end up cutting hair. Not that I would mind. It seems like a really cool job to me, and I'd get to hang out with DiDi more.

"And your real name's Galileo...."

"Yeah," I said. "I guess my family likes to do things pretty different. Kind of weird, huh?"

"No, I...I like different." He looked down, then back up at me again. "Does that mean your mom will ask your sister to name her first kid Delta Dawn, too?"

I was quiet for a second. Trip just made me feel so comfortable, I forgot he didn't know about my whole life. "Well, she—Mama, I mean—died when I was a baby, so she can't really ask."

"I'm sorry."

"Aw, that's okay."

"So you live with your dad?"

"Well." I looked up the hall. The cafeteria was just ahead. I wondered if we would sit together. "He was never in the picture, if you know what I mean. When Mama died, we moved away from Verity to live with our friend Lori a couple of towns over. DiDi got this job sweeping hair at a salon, but now she's a full-time hairdresser and she's really, really good. Everyone says. She never even went to beauty school, because we never had the money for it back—What?"

Trip was studying me again. "Nothing. You're just... you're really... open."

I stopped walking for a second and stood there in the hallway. I wasn't sure if that was a good thing or a bad thing. I was Saying It Like It Is, but maybe this was the kind of town where you keep your mouth shut.

But then he smiled.

And I knew.

It didn't matter what kind of pie I was, Wish or pecan. He just liked me.

I guess it was the perfect moment for another Recipe for Success zinger, but instead, I told him the truth. "Thanks. You—well, you make it really easy. To be open, I mean."

There might have been a second when we both realized that we'd only met that morning and maybe it was kind of weird to get so personal so soon, but then Trip made it easy again and nudged me with an elbow. "So, if that professor was so smart, why didn't he just fix the boat?"

"You know, I asked DiDi the exact same thing."

"What'd she say?"

I remembered how serious she had looked at the time. "She said the real question was why didn't he just build a new one."

"Right... with supplies from the desert island store..." Trip said.

"Or maybe he could have ordered one from the desert island catalog?" I added.

As we walked into that noisy cafeteria together, I made a note to myself that if I was ever stuck on a desert island, I should probably bring someone with survival skills that were a little more practical than DiDi's.

eight

The first thing I noticed was that the cafeteria had all these big bright posters everywhere that said things like U R WHAT U EAT! and HEALTHY KIDZ RULE! I'll tell you right now, my old school had a pretty nice cafeteria. People complained about it, but it looked fine to me. It was huge and the lunch ladies were super-funny—except for this one who worked the cash register and always looked at you cross-eyed like you were hiding an extra buttered roll down your pants. I never had to deal with her, though, because DiDi packed me lunch every single day. She said it saved money and time and I wouldn't have to bother with the cafeteria and all its distractions so I could just go on and find a nice quiet classroom to get my extra-credit work done.

But here, in the Hill Prep cafeteria, I couldn't wait to be distracted. Everywhere, kids were talking and walking and carrying on like it was no big deal to be there. I know the reason DiDi wanted me to work during lunchtime instead of fool around and socialize was so I could get ahead. And that's what I did. Every day for as long as I could remember.

The thing is, when you get that far ahead of everyone else, there's no one left around you.

I tried to keep myself from bouncing nervously as we walked in. Everything was shiny and new. The lunch ladies looked like they should be working at a restaurant. They had on these visors with the school crest on them. There were big windows looking out to fields and trees. And the food...

"That's some salad bar," I said.

Trip wrinkled up his adorable nose. "All these parents complained and got rid of all the junky stuff like Tater Tots and pizza."

"Did someone say Tater Tots?" Billy stuck himself between us, putting an arm around our shoulders. "Tripper, I would disown you for having a mom who led the attack on our beloved deep-fried potato—"

"Except your mom is also on the Healthy Revolution committee."

"Yes," said Billy. "Except for the fact that our moms are working together in this evil plot against a growing boy's right to junk food."

I laughed. Being the new me in this new school was a heck of a lot more fun than I ever imagined it would be.

Billy scanned the room. "C'mon, let's grab a table, before the mutants descend."

Trip looked at me. "I'm buying—are you buying, G-Girl?"

I held up my brown bag.

"Save me a seat, okay?"

"Okay."

I turned to face the crowd, smiling. I was saving sweet, beautiful Trip a seat. I wasn't sure which way to head, but Billy went straight to a table in the back. I followed him, wondering what was it with these boys and the back of the room.

I raised my chin and put a big smile on my face. "Recipe for Success," I whispered to myself. "Recipe for Success."

Billy turned. "You say something?"

"Just...nothing." We had stopped at a table.

"Hey, guys. This is Leia. Aka New Girl. Aka G. Be nice, now. She's got a mean tackle."

I waved. "Hi, everyone."

There were a bunch of boys and girls sitting there. I recognized the girls from class that morning. Chase and Laney. And the one who had been giving me dagger eyes. Mace. Mace Tanglewood. Even though her name didn't sound like it, she looked Chinese or something. She had this crazy sandwich with green sprouts sticking out all over the place and a little toothpick with a flag that said HEALTHY KIDZ R KOOL!

She stared at me but didn't say anything. I sat down a few seats over where I wouldn't have to make eye contact.

I snuck a peek up and down the table, just taking in the buzz and excitement of being there. My very first time sitting with a bunch of kids my age in a cafeteria.

I carefully tore my brown bag open down the center and flattened it out to make a place mat while I listened to the talk around me.

"We're definitely in the best class group this year," Laney was saying. "B Group is so boring. I don't even know anyone in C Group. And D is just—whatever."

Chase was nodding and nodding, her eyes darting between Laney and Mace.

I cleared my throat. "It does seem like a really great group," I said.

There was a second of silence. Chase nodded and smiled at me, then quickly glanced at Mace and Laney like she was checking for permission. Laney looked at me and half-smiled. Mace just stared at her crazy sandwich.

"Yeah," said Billy, unwrapping his lunch. "At least we have the best lunch hour—C group doesn't eat till like one thirty."

"You'd never make it." Trip was standing there with his tray, looking at Billy's row of three giant sandwiches from home.

Billy grinned. "Hey, I'm a growing boy."

Trip sat in the seat I'd saved him. "What's that?"

I looked down at my lunch. On top of my sandwich was

a small folded square of paper. "Oh, that's just a KOB from DiDi."

"A cob?"

"Yeah, but spelled *K, O, B*. It stands for 'Kindness of Bearer.' It's a way to send an important message that's private."

He pointed. "Why does it say this?" *Wait till after lunch to read.*

"Oh, DiDi says the nicest thing you can give a person is something to look forward to." Though I'm not sure why she thinks her KOBs are any great gift. They're the same every day. *Keep up the great work and you will really be something one day!* Or *Study hard and you will be on your way!* For some reason, she thinks telling me that someday, way in the future, I'll turn out okay is something to look forward to.

"Will you show me how to make one?"

"Well, sure. It's easy." I reached into my backpack for a couple of pieces of notepaper. Our heads came close together as I showed him how to do the folds.

"Passing notes, really?" a nasally voice said. "Isn't that kind of immature?" Guess who that came from. Dagger Eyes.

Trip looked at me. Then at his lunch. Then down at his half-folded paper. Everywhere but at Mace.

Billy picked up his second sandwich. "So Trip's hanging with the new girl, Mace. Big deal. You can't always have all the attention."

Mace turned red. The other girls looked at each other, and

the boys coughed into their food. I didn't know what to do. We'd only been sitting there for five minutes. The last thing I wanted on my first day was to be in the middle of some New York private school lunch drama.

"What?" Mace tossed her hair. It flew over her shoulder just like in those shampoo commercials. "She's the one who's dying for all the attention. She gives a whole big speech in class about having a *mama* who's a hairdresser, and she's wearing shoes from the Dollar Store. How did you even get into this school? Are you a scholarship case or something?" She tossed her hair again on the other side.

She was acting like she hated me, and she didn't even know me. I knew what DiDi paid for my education. She'd shown me the bill. We'd applied for scholarships, and I'd received half off the tuition, but what we were still paying was almost half of what DiDi made in a year.

Maybe the old GiGi might not have known what to do, but today, I let Recipe for Success Leia stare Mace down. "Maybe you shouldn't presume what a hairdresser makes. They stay pretty busy with people whose hair"—I did an exaggerated imitation of Mace's hair toss—"is the most important thing on—or in—their heads."

Billy snorted, then stood up. "Okay, weapons down." He leaned in for a quick high five. "Sweet comeback, though, G-Girl—but seriously, time for a new subject: G, what's for lunch? Looks good."

I looked around the table. Everyone else had these big fat grass and hay sandwiches or the hot lunch—which, if you asked me, pretty much looked like broccoli à la broccoli. For the first day of school, DiDi had packed my favorite sandwich in the world. Mama's EZ Cheeze Crunch. It wasn't exactly something you'd find on a Healthy Revolution menu, and for the first time, I found myself wondering if it was an okay thing to bring. I looked over at Trip. He was still focusing all his attention on his half-folded KOB.

This slow smile was spreading across Mace's face as she watched me twist my KOB in my hands. "Wow, I hope it's nothing gross and socially unacceptable," she said. "Like your shoes."

Mama's special sandwich unacceptable? I raised my chin. First day or not, the new Recipe for Success did not let high-and-mighty shampoo-commercial girls put my mama's food down. I pulled my sandwich out and held it up to Mace's face. "Actually, it's the best sandwich on earth. EZ Cheeze with pimentos and potato chips on white, and, last I heard, potatoes were a vegetable. So, you got another one of your little flags for me there? That is, if my sandwich is cool enough for *kool* to be spelled with a *K*."

There was a second of silence at the table. I guess everyone was busy trying to figure out if eating a lunch that probably violated all Ten Commandments in the Healthy Revolution Bible was bigger than the fact that I was friends with Trip and Billy.

Then Billy slowly raised one arm in the air. It took me a second to realize he was trying to give me another high five—which was probably the seventh one that day. "YES. Thank you. Finally, someone on our side to fight the fight! Today EZ Cheeze, tomorrow Tater Tots! Bring back the junk food. Tater…Tots. Tater…Tots! Tater…Tots!" Everyone, except for me, Mace, and Trip, started banging on the table and chanting in unison. "TATER TOTS! TATER TOTS! TATER TOTS!" It caught on for a few seconds around the cafeteria, till everyone broke down, laughing. Billy punched Trip in the shoulder. "Dude, you tripped the right girl."

"W-well, my mom would never let me eat that junk!" Mace said. "EZ Cheeze? That fake orange stuff? It's disgusting. Joke all you want, but—" She pointed at the closest poster. "*U ARE WHAT U EAT.* Which I guess makes you as fake as your cheese."

The laughing stopped. Mace's eyes were like black ice. Then she glanced toward Trip and her face fell for a second before she caught it. I don't know why, but something inside me suddenly thought about how I knew what that was like. Trying to catch a falling face, I mean.

She shoved her grass and hay sandwich away and stood up. "Wish I could stay and talk more about your junky food, but I'm the president of the Seventh Grade Young Entrepreneurs Club—oh, haven't heard of it? Not surprised. It's for people who are going to really make something of themselves.

At least something more than a hairdresser." Then she turned and marched away from the table. The two other girls glanced at each other. Chase gave me a quick nervous look, and then she and Laney both ran after Mace.

Trip glanced over at me. Like he was checking if I was okay. Inside I felt like fake cheese melting in the sun. But my Recipe for Success was telling me to sit up straight, look him right in the eyes, smile, and take a huge bite of my sandwich. I chewed and chewed and swallowed hard.

Like nothing was bothering me at all.

Like I was used to high drama.

Like I hadn't spent every single day of every school year of my life either sitting alone in a classroom, studying during lunch, or hanging out with grown-up librarians who seemed to be the only people interested in getting to know me.

Which kind of made me wonder if that meant I really was as fake as Mace said.

EZ Cheeze Crunch

Pimento Cheese

- 3 cups finely shredded EZ Cheeze brand cheddar
- 2 ounces softened cream cheese
- 3 tablespoons jarred diced pimentos
- 4 tablespoons mayonnaise
- 3 shakes of hot sauce

- Best white bread in town
- Your favorite potato chips

Now, everyone has her own ideas about pimento cheese. Like my good friend Amanda, who just about snorts at this recipe and insists that all a body needs is cheddar, mayo, and a couple little specks of pimento. Well, I say to each her own, but anyone who's had my version *L*, *O*, *V*, *E* loves it.

Put the first 5 ingredients in a nice bowl and work them over with a big wooden spoon till they're mixed together, but still nice and chunky. Cover the bowl with plastic wrap and let it sit in the fridge overnight. I am serious. These things take time.

The next day, take the bowl out, and please do not tell me I have to explain how to make a sandwich.

Just spread that cheese on a piece of bread and then pile on chips and top it with another slice.

And don't forget to serve it with a nice pickle.

Also good with crackers or in grilled cheese sandwiches.

Makes 3 cups. Keeps for up to one week in the fridge.

NINE

Almost all the kids got picked up by their moms after school. I guess so they could go to their harp lessons or stock market classes or whatever. But not me—I walked. Because, like DiDi says over and over and over again, we live in a Walking Town.

Today, though, instead of heading right back to the apartment, I walked to my new job. DiDi had signed me up as a Middle School Library Volunteer. The best part was that afterward, she said, I could stop by the salon, and if she wasn't done yet, I could wait for her a little and watch her talk to people and work. As long as I brought my homework, it should be fine—just this once. It being the first day of school and a special occasion.

When I got to the library, Miss Homer was at the desk on the kids' floor. She also took shifts as a lunch monitor at the cafeteria. Now, the librarians back at my old school were a ton of fun. They were young and funky and thought it was hilarious that I spent more time in the nonfiction section of the library than looking at novels and such. They used to talk a lot about this band they were in that did punk rock versions of these old Saturday-morning cartoon songs about learning and stuff.

Miss Homer didn't exactly seem like the punk rock type. She was dressed in mousy, mousy brown from head to toe, and I'd like to describe her face, but I hadn't seen it yet because her entire head was shoved in a book. Usually, I'd say that made sense for a librarian, except on the cover of this book was a man with long hair blowing in the wind, and he was hugging this lady in a flowy white dress who looked like she was going to up and faint.

"Miss Homer? Hi. I'm G—"

Darn it.

"I—I mean I'm Leia Barnes. Your new volunteer."

Whatever Long-Haired Man and Fainting Lady were up to must have been something else, because Miss Homer stayed glued to that page. "Collect books from the cart. Straighten the toy area." Page turn. "Then Pre-K Storytime. Read something good. Schedule's on the corkboard."

"Um, sure. Thank you, Miss Homer."

It was pretty easy. I picked out a couple of picture books, and boy, those kids just giggled and hugged me and rolled around like life was nothing but a breeze. The moms kept saying how I was adorable with my accent, and a few asked me if I ever did any babysitting. I said sure, I'd been babysitting for years.

Which was kind of true. See, even after DiDi and I got our own place, Lori used to show up in the middle of the night back when she was still drinking—stumbling in, smelling like some kind of fruity cocktail. Mumbling how I was a good girl and she loved me. No matter what time it was, I'd take care of her. Made sure she cleaned up. Got her into bed. Brought her water and an aspirin and set them on the sofa table so she'd see them when she woke up. I used to ask DiDi why Lori didn't come around more often, and she said some people can be there for you all the time and others can't. Just enjoy her while she was around.

When I was done with my volunteer time, I took numbers from all the moms who wanted me to babysit, filled out my little volunteer time card, and left it with Miss Homer. You can guess how excited she was to talk to me again. Page turn. She probably had no idea what I even looked like. But three seconds later, Miss Homer was the last thing on my mind.

As I picked up my backpack, a perfectly folded little KOB fell out with handwriting I'd never seen before.

Wait till you get home to read.

No-Peek Chicken

- 2 tablespoons butter
- 8 chicken thighs (2½ to 3 pounds)
- 1 teaspoon celery salt
- salt and pepper
- 1 large onion, diced (about 2 cups)
- 5 stalks of celery, diced (about 1 cup)
- 2 cups medium-grain rice
- 3½ cups chicken broth

There is nothing I look forward to more than fall comfort food, and I can't think of a better comfort food than chicken and rice. Now, this is how I've been making mine forever.

First, salt and pepper both sides of your chicken thighs and sprinkle the skins with the celery salt. Put your butter in a deep 12-inch skillet over medium-high heat. Add your chicken thighs, browning them skin side up for 5 minutes and then skin side down for 5 more minutes, or until every inch of that skin is golden brown. This is what makes the deep flavor. Add the diced onion and celery to that buttery, chicken-y goodness in the spaces between your chicken pieces, and cook for 5 more minutes, keeping your chicken skin side down. Do not stir. Scatter your rice over top, and then add your broth and turn the heat up to high till everything comes to a boil. Lower to medium, put on a tight-fitting lid, and NO PEEKING for 25 minutes.

After 25 minutes, take off the lid and raise the heat back up to medium-high for 8 minutes. This will crisp up the chicken skin under all that savory rice and make your kitchen smell like heaven. It's okay if the bottom of your rice gets a little golden and crispy, too. That's my favorite part. Just stir it all in and serve.

Now, who wouldn't look forward to that?

Serves 6–8.

ten

think I made that walk back in record time.

Our new little town is what DiDi calls All About the Charm. Which means if you want to buy fancy soap, gourmet jelly, or a big perfume-y candle in a store that looks like it's from an old-fashioned movie, you've come to the right place. But anything practical, like toilet paper or detergent, you have to hop a bus to Super Saver the next town over.

DiDi's salon is on Main Street. It has these huge windows in the front with curly black letters that say SALON DE JEAN RENÉ painted on them. She said the receptionist was named Clarisse and I should just go ahead in, be the polite southern girl she raised me to be, and introduce myself.

Of course, I was still wearing my uniform when I walked

in, but Clarisse greeted me like I was in a mink coat and diamonds. Like she couldn't believe her luck that a real live human seventh grader had just walked in the door.

"Good afternoon and welcome to Salon de Jean René! How may I help you?"

Recipe for Success. I smiled and looked her right in the eyes.

"Hello, are you Miss Clarisse? It's nice to meet you, I'm G—"

Darn it.

"G?" She said. "G! Why, of course! GiGi! Wonderful to meet you. DiDi said you'd be stopping in. She's with a client now, but please go on in and pour yourself a cup of coffee or lemonade, and we have these lovely chocolate chip cookies in the waiting area. Just relax on the divan; she'll be with you in a moment."

"Thank you, Miss Clarisse, wonderful to meet you, too."

I headed for something that looked like a sofa to me but I guess was a divan. I sat down and carefully unzipped my backpack halfway. I reached in and touched the perfect little KOB. It had to be from Trip. Who else could have given it to me? I had already opened DiDi's thrilling KOB that said, *Here's to another straight-A year! You can do it! Just remember what's important!*

I peeked over at DiDi. She looked pretty busy, but I knew better than to offer to help, knowing how fussy she is about me even setting a toe in her work area. I quickly pulled out a work sheet and pencil and started my homework before she looked over. Every once in a while, I gave Trip's KOB a little pat.

When she was finished, DiDi introduced me around. There were a bunch of super-nice ladies and Shane, this man who could give DiDi's Beautiful Gay Best Friend, Harley, a run for his money. Jean, the owner, came over and kissed my hand. There were a few other people, but we just waved at them while DiDi pointed to me and called out, "This is my brilliant little sister, G"—I glared at her—"I mean—uh—Leia!"

She headed out the door with me, pulling on her sweater and apologizing. "Sorry! Sorry! Sorry! But honestly, GiGi—dang, I mean Your Royal Highness Princess Earmuffs—how am I supposed to change what's been stuck in my head for the last twelve years?"

"Just please, please try," I said.

"Fine, I'll try. Now hush! We're on full Kenneth Alert."

We walked three steps to the entrance of our apartment. DiDi closed the door softly behind her. We had made it all the way to the top step when *creeeak!*—and just like that, Kenneth's door flew open.

"Hi, Kenneth. Fancy meeting you here," said DiDi with a sigh.

I gave him a little wave. I feel sorry for poor old ponytailed Kenneth, so I always make sure I'm nice to him. He's just awkward and smitten with DiDi like everyone else on the planet.

Kenneth shuffled his feet. "Um..."

"Well, will you look at the time? Nice chatting, Kenneth! See you."

When we were safe inside, she looked at me and crossed her eyes. I felt bad, but I couldn't help laughing. Then she asked about my first day, and I told her about school and classes, and, oh, I met a boy.

"A boy? You met a boy? What boy? Which boy? Where? When? Why?"

"Grammatical much, DiDi? Geez, calm down," I said. "No one's getting married or anything. I just met a boy. If you're going to get all technical about it, I met about a hundred boys—and girls, too. So no big deal. Did you ever hear of something called Making Friends? Most big sisters are happy when their little sisters do it."

"Okay. Fine. Calm yourself," DiDi said. "You met some nice girls? Why don't you tell me about them? Do they get good grades?"

Typical DiDi.

"Sure, I can tell you about the nice girls. Do you want to hear about the nice Chinese girl who already hates me and called me a big fake at lunch?"

"Wait! What? Who hates you?"

"ARGH! Never mind! It's no big deal. I can handle it. I did handle it."

DiDi took a deep breath. "Okay, Double G—sorry, I mean LEIA. I did not mean to make you feel like you can't have friends. Of course you can have friends. Girls and—if you have to—boys, too. I just don't want you to get distracted, okay? We have a plan, remember. There is no way I'm letting you end up cutting hair like me."

"Yeah, working in a beautiful place and helping people look good and feel better about themselves all day? Fate worse than death, D."

"Stop it, G, you know what I mean."

"I know, I know."

"And about that girl calling you fake? You just put that out of your mind. Remember: When people call you names, they're saying more about themselves than they are about you."

More wisdom from the great DiDi.

"Just forget it, D."

"Okay. It's forgotten. Get out your books. But about that boy—"

"DiDi—geez! I told you, it's no big deal."

No, meeting Trip wasn't a big deal.

It was a huge deal.

eleven

I went straight to my room to start homework.

At least that's what I told DiDi.

What I really did was lock the door and then pull out the KOB. *Wait till you get home to read.* I'd kept my promise.

I opened it.

> *Did you wait till you got home? Haha. Just kidding.*
> *I just wanted to say I'm sorry if lunch was weird. I'm*
> *glad you moved here. I really, really like you and liked*
> *talking. See you tomorrow, T*

I traced over the words with their perfectly dotted *i*'s and neat little *o*'s. A boy sent me a KOB. And not just any boy. Trip. The most beautiful, sweetest boy ever. He went to all the trouble to make it for me and then slip it into my backpack.

He said *really* two times. He really, really liked me. And he was glad I moved here. At that very second, so was I.

So was I.

I've kind of just always done whatever DiDi asked me to, so when she said we were moving, I started packing. Leaving the South was a big deal for DiDi. She had it in her head that unless she got me out of that trailer park, I wouldn't have a future. It didn't matter to her that I was happy there and that we had the nicest neighbors, who all looked out for each other.

"The North Shore," she said, eyes all shiny and bright. "That's on Long Island, New York, G. Remember Lori's boyfriend who sold supplies to all the schools? He said New York is where the best schools in the country are, and—c'mon!— we could be living on an island! Beaches and boats and water."

There were plenty of beaches in South Carolina. All you had to do was hop in the car, so I don't think that was the big deal. And of all the places we could go, I didn't get why DiDi would pick somewhere called the North Shore, which, if you ask me, sounded like it'd be the exact opposite of the South.

Oh, she talked a big talk about moving, but moving takes money, and that was one thing we never seemed to have enough of.

Then DiDi heard about the Mayflower Bake-Off.

It's this nationwide contest where you have to come up with a recipe that uses products in the Mayflower family. Which is just a ton of stuff like refrigerator biscuits, cake mixes, and such. It's a pretty big deal and they have all these categories to enter. Then they pick a Grand Prize, and the winner gets one million dollars. I swear. DiDi decided to go for the Dinner Delights category and then she went straight into Mama's Cookbook "for research."

I thought she should make something like a beautiful dessert or hors d'oeuvre (which is just a fancy word for appetizer). But DiDi said this contest was going to change our lives and she wanted to go with something special.

And that's how she decided to enter Mama's Turn Over a New Leaf Turnovers. Even the name was perfect. It was for when you found yourself in a sad situation with a whole heap of leftover chicken and wanted to make something amazing out of it.

She won.

Everyone loved it, and I swear that for the rest of the summer, everyone we knew made Mama's Turn Over a New Leaf Turnovers. I figured that million dollars would change our lives forever.

That was when the crazy part started.

Before she'd let them take the official winner's photo, DiDi had her Beautiful Gay Best Friend, Harley, give her a total makeover. New hair, face—everything. Even I couldn't recognize her. Then she said that, for reasons of a delicate nature, her real name was not to be used anywhere in print, but that she'd be glad to provide a suitable alias. Well, the good people at Mayflower had their winning recipe, so they said she could call herself whatever she wanted. At first, I thought it was all pretty fun and glamorous, but then DiDi just ended up using Lori's name and giving her some of the prize money for her trouble. Now, I have no problem sharing with Lori— she practically saved our lives way back when we needed a place to stay. But if you're going to get a total makeover and play the name game, why not go all out? She could've been anyone.

"Anytime you make up a story, G, it's best to have a little bit of truth to it. Otherwise it's hard to keep track of things. All I want is to make sure we have our privacy. This money is nobody's business but ours."

If you asked me, with a million dollars, we should've thrown a big old celebration for the neighborhood. We should be living in a mansion with a butler and a pet tiger and a swimming pool filled with champagne. But then DiDi started in on how a million dollars was not all that much money. Even with my scholarship. How she still had to pay taxes and with six more years of private school and then college, it wouldn't even end up being enough. Yakkity. Yakkity. Yak. Can you imagine? A million dollars not enough money?

Everyone knows I'm the math whiz in the family, but DiDi is the legal guardian, so she gets the final say. I'll tell you what, though, if I ever got my hands on some of that money, the first thing I'd buy DiDi is a calculator.

So here we are. No big fancy house. No swimming pool. Just living the way we always did. The only thing she was going to spend a penny on was My Future. The money, DiDi said, was to make sure I got to be what I deserved to be. Getting fancy wasn't going to do it, but making sure I got educated was.

"But, D, wouldn't it be nice to at least have a new car?" I said, looking at the Blue Bomb with its funny back fins and headlight eyes. "This poor thing is practically prehistoric!"

"When would we use it, G? I work right downstairs and you can walk to school. Besides, the Blue Bomb got us where we needed to go. She deserves to retire as a permanent member of the family and relax. I'm done with driving. Besides, now we live in a—"

"Walking Town. I know, I know...."

I think the real reason DiDi doesn't like to drive a lot is because she hates her driver's license photo. I mean, she does all this talking about what's really important and what's silly, but truth is DiDi can be downright vain. She says it's the worst picture of anybody in the history of everything and won't even let me see it—which honestly I could give a hoot about. I'll bet if she ever got pulled over by the police and had to pull it out, she'd start crying. Good-looking people sure can be crazy. It kind of makes me glad to be just okay.

I looked at Trip's KOB and read it about a hundred more times. Then I carefully folded it back up and put it in an old shoe box and stuck it way up on a high shelf in our closet where DiDi keeps all these old papers and records. Then took it back down and snapped a big rubber band around the whole thing. And then another and another. That KOB was my private business, and all I know is that if DiDi found a note from a boy saying how he really, really liked me, she would go really, really Grammatical.

My Turn Over a New Leaf Turnovers

Million-Dollar Bacon

- 8 tablespoons light brown sugar
- 1 teaspoon cayenne pepper
- 1 package (1 pound) thick-sliced bacon

Turnover Filling

- 1 pound cooked chicken
- 2 tablespoons butter
- ½ cup tiny-diced carrots
- ½ cup tiny-diced onions
- ½ cup tiny-diced celery
- ½ cup tiny frozen sweet green peas
- 1 small can (11 ounces) Mayflower condensed Cream of Chicken Soup
- About 11 ounces half-and-half (enough to fill the soup can)
- Salt and pepper

Turnovers

- 1 egg
- 1 tablespoon milk
- 2 packages Mayflower empanada dough

Sometimes you find yourself in a mess. Whole pile of dry chicken and no idea what to do. Well, just Turn Over a New Leaf.

Anyone can say they make a nice turnover or even a chicken pot pie, but my turnovers are the only ones with my special Million-Dollar Bacon.

Preheat your oven to 400°F. Mix together your brown sugar and cayenne. Set your bacon strips flat on a foil-covered nice cooking sheet. Then, one at a time, put a spoonful of the sugar mixture on each slice and spread it evenly over the top. Carefully flip each one over and repeat on the other side. When all your slices are coated, put the sheet in the oven for 15 to 20 minutes, till the bacon is sizzling and dark golden brown. Let it cool for just a minute, then put the slices on a plate to rest before they get too stiff and stuck to the pan.

Then take two big forks and shred your chicken. Put the butter in a pan over medium-high heat. Sauté your carrots, onions, and celery till they're nice and soft, about 10 minutes. Add the peas and chicken and your can of soup.

Fill the empty soup can with your half-and-half and add that, too. Let everything warm up together, then lower the heat. Salt and pepper to taste.

Beat the egg and the milk in a small bowl. Now take your empanada dough disks and put a nice big spoonful of your chicken filling on each piece, a little to one side and leaving a ½-inch border. Break up your Million-Dollar Bacon into pieces and cover the chicken mixture with it. And don't be shy, because that Million-Dollar Bacon is what gives those turnovers a real kick.

Dampen the edges of each empanada with the egg wash and fold the dough over. This is the pretty part. Crimp the edges all around with a fork and score the top with a knife till it looks just like a beautiful leaf. Brush the tops with the egg wash. Bake on lightly greased cookie sheets in the 400°F oven till golden brown, about 15 minutes. Turn the pans halfway through.

Makes 10 to 12, depending on how fat you stuff them.

Trust me. They taste like a million bucks.

Enjoy!

twelve

After the first few weeks of school, I was already happier than I ever thought I could be. Trip and I spent all our time together. He loved all my stories about DiDi and Lori and the funny things that happened back in South Carolina. I talked and talked, and he listened and left me KOBs. I treasured every last one.

Haha! I liked that story you told today.

Where do you get golden bullets, anyway?

I think you're the first person I've ever really felt like I could talk to.

I'm glad you're here.

Each one was marked *Wait till you get home to read,* so I had something to look forward to before I started my homework.

The only thing that didn't thrill me was that hanging out with Trip and Billy meant I had to hang out with Mace and her friends. Chase was nice to me every once in a while when she forgot maybe she wasn't supposed to be, but I have to admit, whenever I was around them, I'd get this little twinge inside. Those girls were together all the time. Sitting together and giggling and walking around with their arms linked and their friendship bracelets flashing. It made me wish I had some girlfriends of my own.

Someone I could talk to about boys.

Someone I could go to when I wanted to ask questions like: What do you do when you really, really like someone and they tell you they really, really like you, too? Not to mention they send you secret notes all the time. Does it mean you're boyfriend and girlfriend? The only girl I ever hung out with was DiDi, and there was no way that talk was ever going to happen with her.

So I was really looking forward to the Club & Activities Fair. I knew there was a club that Mr. McGuire thought I should join, but mostly I was thinking that if I looked for clubs I liked, I'd probably find a couple of girlfriends I liked, too. There were four seventh-grade class groups at Hill Prep, and so far, I really only knew one of them.

The day of the fair, I walked into the field house (which is just a fancy name for a gym) and it was packed with students. There was every kind of club you could imagine. Sports

Boosters. Mathletes. Theater. School Paper. Arts Magazine. Robotics Club. Each one had big signs in bright letters. You could tell some of the tables were the popular ones and others were quiet.

And then I noticed a small table to the side.

The Stargazers.

My hand reached up and touched the star on my forehead.

"Hey, G! G-Girl!"

I looked around. It was Billy over at the Sports Boosters Club, which was the table with the biggest crowd. They actually had three tables pushed together and a giant banner flying overhead. Trip was standing there, smiling. He gave me a little wave and beckoned me over. He looked so cute in his soccer uniform, kicking a ball around with kids from the boys' and girls' teams. Everyone was laughing, and the girls looked fun with their pretty ponytails flipping around. It was a no-brainer for my Recipe for Success.

I started toward Trip, then stopped and glanced back at the Stargazers. Just two girls, sitting there, huddled together. The homemade poster taped to the front of their table was decorated with shiny stars and words in the shapes of constellations. Someone opened the double doors that led outside, and the poster flew up and tore away from the table. I ran over to help. I held it for a second and it was like something electric was running through my fingertips.

"Hi," I said, handing the poster over, and, before I realized it, I was saying, "Can I join?" I looked down at the signup sheet. It was handwritten on this black construction paper in silvery marker. There were just three names on the list: *Haven Chang* and *Allie Middleton* and *Faculty Advisor: Mr. McGuire*.

"R-really?" said one of the girls. She was wrestling with the tape, trying to get the poster to stay on the table. "I mean, sure. It's—it's still early—that's why we don't really have anyone else yet, but I think we'll get more. And—um—we do a lot of really cool stuff, like trips to the observatory—midnight campouts, museums, movies...lots of stuff. Cool stuff. It's—it's really cool."

She seemed kind of like one of those nervous types, standing there reciting all her club facts, but I liked the look of her. She had this nose with a sort of bump. DiDi calls them Just You Wait Noses. Meaning when she's older, she'll go from kind of awkward to totally beautiful in a really different and glamorous way. I nodded to both girls. "Hi, I'm G—"

Dang it all.

"G?" the girl with the nose asked.

I sighed. "I mean Leia."

"Oh. Hi. I'm Haven."

"I'm Allie," the other girl chimed in. She had a really smiley face with dimples. She was strapping enough tape on her side of the poster to keep it there for all eternity.

"Well, it's really nice to meet you both," I said, and I picked up that pretty silvery pen and wrote my name on the list. *Leia Barnes.* Seeing it there in my curliest cursive, surrounded by those sparkling constellations, I thought it looked just right.

"Well, well, look who's gazing at stars. How very appropriate." Mr. McGuire stepped up to the table, looking pleased.

Both girls smiled and the air around us just seemed to become relaxed and comfortable the way things always did when Mr. McGuire was around. I was glad to know he was part of it.

"Fellow Stargazers, keep up the recruiting. I'm going to run and break up that little tussle at the Mathletes table. You know the kind of burgeoning criminal minds that come out of that lot." He saluted us and took off.

"G-Girl!" I looked up. Billy was still flagging me down and Trip was looking over at the Stargazers table. I waved and turned to go. "Okay, just let me know when we have meetings or something," I said to Haven and Allie.

Both girls had stopped smiling. It wasn't too hard to figure out why. With me and Mr. McGuire leaving, the population of their club was about to be cut in half.

"Are you the girl who tripped over Trip the first day of school?" Allie asked.

"No—yes, I kind of—" I gave up. "Yeah, that was me."

Gossip again. I was trying to figure out if it was the nice kind or the Dead Drunk Donna kind, when Allie said, "You're so lucky. He's definitely the cutest boy in school. Is he totally into you now?"

My face reddened. "Oh, I don't know...."

I really, really like you.

Was he?

"I bet he is! Don't you guys hang out all the time?"

I think I got even redder. Haven rescued me. "Did you write your number? We'll let you know when we start meetings."

"Thanks. I am really, really glad I signed up." And I was. Just because I didn't like my name didn't mean I wasn't going to try and be a scientist like Mama would've wanted. I thought about the breeze that had blown that poster practically into my hands. Like part of Mama just wanted me to be a Stargazer. It was almost magical.

"G!"

I didn't want to break the spell of that feeling, but I moved toward the Sports Boosters.

There were shouts of "Hi, G!"

Mace crossed her arms. "What did you just sign up for? Not the Mutants from Mars, I hope."

Trip was talking and joking with a bunch of the boys and didn't hear.

Mace cleared her throat and spoke up again. "Uh, Galileo, was that the Mutants from Mars table I just saw you at? Your hairdresser mama will be so proud."

I saw Trip turn toward us. Billy leaned over to see what was going on.

The magical feeling of Mama I was holding on to disappeared, and my throat suddenly got tight. I was used to Mace putting me down, but I didn't have a snappy comeback today. I'd only told Trip all about Mama being gone, and I wasn't sure if I was ready to have everyone know, but I couldn't stop myself.

"Before my mama died, she always wanted to study the stars, and I just—" I straightened up and looked Mace in the eyes. "I just want to follow in her footsteps." It sure didn't sound like something that would come out of any Recipe for Success. It wasn't snappy or zingy. But it was the truth.

Mace opened her mouth and then shut it.

I guess Dead Mama territory is a place even mean girls won't go.

"Your mom died? That's so sad," said Chase. "I'm sorry."

Laney glanced at Mace, then gave me a small smile and nodded at me.

Trip was watching me.

There was this little ring of silence around us in that big, noisy crowd.

"Well, I think it's cool that you're following in your mom's footsteps," Billy said. Then he shoved his hands into his pockets and grinned. "I'm going to follow in my dad's footsteps and collect Mustang convertibles."

Everyone sort of started laughing in relief. Billy looked

at me with kind eyes, then raised his hand in a gentle little high five.

I took a deep breath and turned toward Trip. He reached out like he was going to give my arm a squeeze and slipped a folded KOB into my hand.

That night for dinner, DiDi made Mama's Maybe Even Better Soup. If you live where snapping turtles are, then making snapper soup is about as easy as catching one, which I can tell you is not all that easy. You have to find a big, strong stick so they don't bite you, and boy, can they bite. I mentioned Davey Dylan and his missing pinky finger. Well, Davey says all you have to do is take the stick and hold it out and when that snapper stretches his neck out and chomps down on it—*whack!*—you take his head off with an axe.

I'm not big on whacking things with an axe.

And seeing as there's no 24-hour snapping turtle store out here, DiDi always makes Mama's special snapping turtle soup that has no snapping turtle in it.

When we were done eating, DiDi said, "Dang, no finger—you get a finger?"

Maybe Even Better Soup

Roux

- ½ cup vegetable oil
- ½ cup flour

Soup

- 2 tablespoons olive oil
- 1 cup yellow onion, diced small
- 1 cup red bell pepper
- ½ cup celery, diced small
- ½ cup carrot, diced small
- 1 teaspoon Italian seasoning
- 1 teaspoon cayenne pepper
- 2 teaspoons salt
- 1 tablespoon garlic, minced
- 3 cups crushed canned tomatoes (from a 28-ounce can)
- 1 pound hamburger meat
- 4 cups chicken stock
- 2 tablespoons lemon juice
- 2 bay leaves
- 2 tablespoons flat (Italian) parsley, chopped
- Salt and pepper
- 4 hard-boiled eggs, chopped

Now, this is just about the fanciest thing you'll find in here. My mama's best friend said she had this soup with the mayor's wife's sister once, and I don't think you can get much fancier than that.

First make your roux, and don't get all worried about it. It's pronounced *roo*, and it's just a little something to help give your soup a little body. (And what girl can argue with that?) Brown your flour in the oil in a small saucepan over medium heat, stirring constantly so it doesn't burn. In about 10 minutes, it'll turn a nice caramel brown. Take it off the stove and let the poor thing rest in a fresh container to cool off.

Into a big soup pot put 1 tablespoon olive oil and cook your onions, peppers, celery, carrots, Italian seasoning, cayenne, and 1 teaspoon salt for about 15 minutes, till the veggies are completely soft and tender.

Add the garlic and tomatoes and cook for 10 more minutes.

Add your hamburger meat and another teaspoon of salt and cook, you guessed it, 10 minutes more. Then add your chicken stock, lemon juice, bay leaves, and parsley, and bring to a simmer.

Add your roux little by little until the soup is as thick and grand as gravy. Pepper and salt to taste. Simmer 15 more minutes. Take out the bay leaves. Serve in bowls with chopped egg on top.

It may not be snapper soup, but you know, I think it may be even better.

Serves 4.

thirteen

The very next day, the phone rang.

Which was pretty exciting. I mean, since we'd moved here, I'd only gotten two phone calls. Both from Lori. Just checking in and seeing how we were doing. I figured she'd want to come and visit or something, but DiDi said we had to understand that people can't always be what you want. Lori had her own things to attend to. We only saw her every month or two before we moved, so I guess nothing had really changed.

This time, when I picked up the phone, there was this pause. The kind where you know someone is there. They just haven't figured out what to say yet.

"Hello?" I said. "This is the Barnes residence."

"Um . . ."

And just like that, I knew it was Haven Chang from the Stargazers.

"Hi, Haven!" I said. "How are you?"

"Oh, um, hi, Leia."

"So . . ."

"So . . . I, um, I didn't realize this was your house—I texted you first—and then the text didn't go through. . . ."

"Oh, I know. It's so crazy. DiDi—that's my big sister—she has this whole thing where she doesn't think I need a cell phone—so I'm, like, what? The only kid on the whole planet now who doesn't have one?" I laughed. Another great DiDi idea making my life crazy.

Haven giggled for a second. "Yeah. My, uh, my parents have really weird rules, too. Like even on days the maid comes, I still have to make my own bed and clean my room."

"Yup . . . That's crazy, all right," I agreed. And then, for no particular reason, we both laughed like it was the best joke ever.

Then it got quiet again.

"So . . . have you been friends with Allie a long time?" I asked. I pictured them running around together in little diamond-covered diapers.

"We met in fourth grade when her mom came to work with my mom at Face Place."

"Face who?"

Haven giggled. "Face Place. Haven't you ever been? It's the best, best makeup store in New York City. They have everything!"

"Everything?"

"Yeah. You could come in sometime—if you want. My mom is the buyer, and she lets us have all these free samples and—even makeovers."

I took a breath. "Do you have..."

Haven waited. Then said, "What? If they don't have it, my mom will know how to get it."

I shook my head.

"Nothing," I said.

We decided that the first official meeting of the Stargazers would be the next day in the science room after school.

"Mr. McGuire is the best advisor," Haven said as we waited for him. "He makes sure we know all about the cool things like shooting stars and stuff."

"Shooting stars." I liked the sound of that. I wasn't sure if DiDi would approve of me spending time just looking at stars and not learning enough to cement my place in the Halls of Greatness, but I thought maybe Mama would've liked it.

"I think it sounds perfect."

Mr. McGuire walked in. "Well, if it isn't the famous Miss

Galileo." He shook my hand as if I were the most important guest he could ever imagine having over. "Good to have you here."

On the first day of class after roll call, Mr. McGuire had started doing these magic tricks. The first one was a total fake-out. Meaning that it was a trick that didn't work and put us off our game. So we all figured he couldn't do any tricks at all and was setting us up to think he was just a young, friendly, goofy teacher. But then the next thing you know, he started doing stuff like finding a card in his shoe with Trip's exact signature on it when we had all watched Trip rip up that card and throw it away. Guess there was more to Mr. McGuire than he first let on. I like people like that. People who have more to them than they let you see right away.

No one else came. It was just Haven and Allie and Mr. McGuire, and that was just fine with me. We talked about what our goals were. What kinds of things we wanted to see. Haven wanted to visit the observatory in the city. Allie wanted to go to the North Pole and see the Northern Lights, which Mr. McGuire mentioned might be a smidge over our budget.

"And what about our newest member, the aptly named Miss Galileo? What would you like this unlikely gathering of dreamers and explorers to do for you?"

What could I say?

That if I searched the stars long and hard enough, maybe— just maybe—I'd find the part of me that came from Mama?

"I don't know," I said. "I just want to find...something amazing."

"Living up to the name, no doubt." Mr. McGuire reached out and spun the little solar system model on the desk. As it went around and around, he gestured about the room filled with shiny cutout stars and constellation maps and said, "The universe is yours, Miss Galileo. Welcome."

fourteen

Miracle of miracles, DiDi agreed to let me take babysitting jobs from the moms at the library as long as I kept my perfect grades. It was my very first time with a real paying job. Come to think of it, it was the very first time for a lot of things.

It was the first time I had spending money of my own, and with what these moms were paying me to watch their cute kids and sit in their beautiful houses, I was able to get myself some really nice clothes like I'd always wanted. I mean, I had the uniform to get me through the school week, but the weekends were a different story, because now I had people to see and places to go.

It was also the first time that I wasn't being completely truthful with DiDi.

A couple of times on Saturday mornings, she'd ask me if I wanted to help her plan the Gala menu, and I'd tell her I was going to study at the library. But then I'd stow my stuff away in the children's coat closet and double back and meet Trip and everyone in town for a day of Absolutely No Studying. Just Fun.

Living in a Walking Town meant we could go anywhere we wanted anytime. I could walk from our apartment to school, to the library, to this cute little boutique with the prettiest clothes I'd ever seen in my life. But best of all, I could walk to the movies, and that was Trip's favorite thing to do. We'd go to this great old movie theater that always had Saturday movie marathons. Trip loved old horror movies the best. I didn't always get to sit next to him, but that was all right. There was always a big group of us. I was just good and glad to be there. I didn't even mind that Mace would toss her perfect hair and give me the death stare whenever Trip wasn't looking.

Even school days were fun for the first time. I still got all my top grades, though I had to stay up later at home to get all my extra credit done, since my days of studying during lunchtime were over. But DiDi didn't need to know that. Or that I spent all my study halls and free time talking to Trip about, oh, everything in the world. He listened and listened and didn't always say much himself, but that was okay. I had plenty of KOBs to open up at home, telling me that even though he wasn't good at saying stuff out loud, he still wanted to let me know how he felt. DiDi's KOBs, on the other hand, I'd stopped opening, dropping them in the garbage on my way out of the cafeteria. It's not like they were ever going to say anything new.

One day, Mr. McGuire was writing on the board when we walked into the classroom. Trip swung into his seat like he always did, and I looked at him like having a beautiful, rumply boy want to sit next to me every single day was the most natural thing in the world. Billy hurled himself into the seat on my other side and gave me a wide grin.

"Hey, Tripper! Hey, G!"

I gave Billy his hourly high five that I'm pretty sure he would shrivel up and die without. Then Trip laughed at us and as I turned back to him and looked into his Wish Pie eyes, I just wanted to tell him everything about how I felt inside and how I had never in my life even come close to liking a boy like him who sent me sweet notes who maybe or maybe not was my boyfriend, and if only I could tell him—

"*The Truth!*" Mr. McGuire bellowed, pointing to the huge words he had just written.

I jumped about a foot in the air, which made both Billy and Trip just lose it. Mr. McGuire never gets mad, though. He just started passing out papers, calm as can be.

"Ladies and gentlemen, we have started our preparations

for landing. Please make sure your tray tables and seat backs are in the upright position, so we can begin our talk about the Truth. In literature and poetry."

Right away, I could feel myself starting to think about other stuff. See, I've never really been into reading a lot of stories and poems. My librarian friends at my old school used to make suggestions all the time, but DiDi prefers I don't waste time with daydreaming and nonsense. She figures that the arts are just not the direction I should take my Recipe for Success. That science is more the road for me. Even though I was making up my own Recipe from now on, I had to agree with her about that. After all, it was in my blood and it was the part of Mama that was a part of me. I wasn't about to let that go.

"Ponder this, O brilliant pupils: Is writing fiction no more than lying? Making up a story so real, so full of true feeling that while we read, we can only accept it as true? At least within its context. Beautiful lies. But lies nonetheless." Mr. McGuire strolled to the window and gazed off into the distance, like maybe the rest of his lecture was out there by the football field. I started thinking about the extra credit I could ask for in math later.

"Now...poetry, on the other hand. Many would argue that to speak poetry is to speak the Truth. A truth so beautiful it makes the heart hurt with its honesty. Please look at the papers I've put on your desks while I read 'This Is Just to Say':

I have eaten
the plums
that were in
the icebox

and which
you were probably
saving
for breakfast

Forgive me
they were delicious
so sweet
and so cold

"Penned by the inimitable William Carlos Williams. Now compare that to—someone give me an example of your favorite book—ah yes! Always ready with an answer, Mr. Billy Fender?"

"My algebra book. I always cry at the part where you don't know what *x* stands for." Billy pretended to blow his nose.

The class laughed, as always.

Mr. McGuire wiped an imaginary tear from his eye and

flicked it into the air. "Ah yes. A classic tragedy..." And that is why he is hands down my favorite teacher. Back home, a smart aleck like Billy would be in the principal's office after that. "Anyone else? Someone less sentimental, perhaps? How about Misssssss Galileo!"

Mr. McGuire has yet to call me Leia. He said he loved the name Galileo and he just had to meet the mom who was creative enough to give it to me. He turned red when I told him that wasn't going to happen, seeing as Mama was dead. I didn't mean to make him feel bad; I was just Saying It Like It Is. He said sorry and that she must have been an extraordinary woman, and I replied that she was.

"Miss Galileo? We await your response with bated breath."

Darn. "Uh, me?" I said. Because, remember, I like to come up with really snappy zingers.

"Uh, you, Miss Galileo," Mr. McGuire said. "In your humble scientific opinion, does poetry lie or tell the truth?"

I thought about it. "Well... isn't it all lies?" I asked. "Aren't you just trying to entertain people when you write stories or poetry—or, you know, whatever?"

"Or-you-know-whatever." Mr. McGuire pretended to pull a knife out of his heart. "Miss Galileo, clarify your point. Are you saying William Carlos Williams was simply trying to entertain someone with the story of eating the cold plums instead of expressing a deep truth?"

"Well, maybe none of that ever happened, and he just

presented it that way because he wanted to look good. He probably just wanted people to think he was something he wasn't."

"Or perhaps, Miss Galileo, he wanted to take something painful from his past—stealing plums—and turn it into something beautiful—a poem."

I shrugged. "Maybe...but I don't know why he has to make it all stretched out and funny-looking on the paper. He should just Say It Like It Is."

"Alas, I believe we have a realist on our hands, but one with her own style of debate. So I will let your argument stand in light of the fact that we will have an assignment in which each of you will come up with your own answer. This semester we search for the Truth." He pointed to the words on the chalkboard again. "What is your Truth? Reflect upon it. Write it. This assignment will be due in four weeks."

Everyone cheered.

"During which there will still be regularly assigned homework...."

Everyone booed.

"And your Truth will be written in the form of poetry."

The booing went up in volume.

"Put away the pitchforks and torches, O angry villagers," Mr. McGuire said. He's the only teacher I know who won't even blink at a room full of booing students. "Poetry takes time. I want you to think—dare I say, ruminate—for a while. Take notes. Live with it. For those of you in need of a definition for *ruminate*, please see Mr. Fender."

I raised my hand. "Can we do an essay or a report or maybe research a poet instead?"

Mr. McGuire studied me for a moment before answering. "Sorry, Miss Galileo, but it looks like you're going to have to search the stars for inspiration. Now, everyone, I want to see Truth on the page. Show me this and make way for a life filled with riches, fame, and high marks in English."

Trip was watching me in that special way he had. "This is a really good one for you."

"Me? Why? I don't like poetry."

"Well...you always tell the truth, and now...now all you have to do is make it rhyme or something."

Billy leaned in toward us. "This is just to say I wish you could get your sister, DiDi, to pack an extra fried chicken and butter sandwich. They look so...uh, fried and salty, and all I'll probably get to eat is a Healthy Revolution Tomato. Forgive me. I already stole your lunch."

Then he held up the brown bag he had snuck from my backpack. I laughed and grabbed it back. Knowing people like Trip and Billy was the best part of moving here, but I did have to disagree with Billy on one thing. There is nothing in all the world better than a true summer tomato.

Because it never needs to become anything else to be the best it can be. No fancy frying or shish-kabobbing or anything like that.

It is what it is.

And that's just fine with me.

True Summer Tomato

- The best homegrown summer tomato you can pick
- Salt

That's it. A tomato and salt.

Now, you all calm down. As long as there are ingredients, this is a recipe.

Pick the tomato warm from the garden.

Sit right there in a sunny patch if you've got one.

Brush off any dirt and bugs, but don't make yourself crazy.

Sprinkle with a little salt. And don't you dare add one other thing, because there's just something about a tomato being a tomato. Eat it like an apple. Let the juices run down your chin, and then wipe 'em away with your shirtsleeve. You heard me. The perfect summer tomato is worth half a shirt.

And that's the truth.

Serves 1.

fifteen

Do you want to come over and hang out at my house after school...just you and me?"

I stared at Trip in surprise.

We were always together during the school day. We sat by each other in all our classes and at lunch, and we walked together in the halls. But never without a crowd of our friends around us. We had never hung out, just the two of us, before.

"G-Girl."

I was still staring. All I could say was, "Wha—huh?" Because, don't forget, I'm pretty smooth with the comebacks.

"I don't have soccer, so we can hang out all afternoon. Do you...want to?"

"Well, I do. I do. Really. I do. But—uh, I better call DiDi

and find out what her plans are because I—I might have to meet up with her after school...." Or I might have to run for my life when I tell her I want to hang out at a boy's house by myself in a situation that has absolutely nothing to do with my academic advancements.

"She works at Jean René's, right?" Mace had caught up with us in the hall. "I wonder what it's like to have your hands in someone's dirty hair all day."

It didn't take me long to add up that, in Mace's snot-nosed opinion, DiDi being a hairdresser is not the same as everyone else's working moms and dads. Mace's mom runs all these charity balls. Trip told me that his mom doesn't work, but she plays tennis like any day she's going to get the call to play in front of the Queen of England. I've always loved that DiDi is a hairdresser like Mama, but for the first time, I felt funny that she had to shampoo other people's dirty hair and sweep it off the floor. I wondered what Trip was thinking.

But I raised my chin, because my Recipe for Success says never to show when someone's getting to you. "DiDi loves being a hairdresser, and she's really great at it, too. She just has a way of making people feel comfortable and happy, and she makes them look better than they did before. It's a lot more than most people do in their jobs." I steadied the shake in my voice.

Mace didn't give up. "But you guys live over the salon? In one of those creepy old apartments? I hear they don't even have heat in the winter. Doesn't it smell like shampoo half the time?"

"Good thing I like the smell of shampoo, then."

Trip was watching the ground and biting his lip. He turned toward me a little. Putting his shoulder between me and Mace. Like a protective wall. "C'mon, let's . . . let's just go," he said in a low voice.

Mace looked back and forth between us. Then she raised her chin and walked away.

Walking through town with Trip, I thought about how easily he had folded me into his group. Sometimes when DiDi makes peanut butter cookies, she'll get all cranky trying to blend the peanut butter into the sugar, eggs, and butter. See, the peanut butter always stays in a big clump and the eggs are all slimy and you have to really work at it before everything gets nice and smooth. But the way Trip pulled me into his buttery, sugary life, you'd never even know I was peanut butter in the first place.

When we got to Main Street, we stopped at the Sweet Home Bakery, where Trip treated us to these beautiful cookies. I'd never ever had a cookie like this in my life. Especially coming out of anyone's home, no matter how sweet it was. The icing was smooth and shiny with these pretty little pearls dotting the top. Trip bought one for DiDi, too. Even though it was only one cookie, they put it in a tiny box with a ribbon. It looked like a perfect little present.

"You don't have to do that!" I said.

"My mom is raising me to be a gentleman." He held the door to the salon open for me.

"Well, good luck with that! Did you forget that DiDi and I are from the South? Holding doors is just the beginning. Just don't take anything personally," I quickly added. "DiDi is overprotective. She doesn't really like to let me hang out with—I mean, I don't think she really wants me, um, having a boy who is a friend."

"Don't worry, grown-ups always love me. They think I'm... the perfect kid or something."

All I can say is if every grown-up in the universe thought I was perfect, I'd look a lot happier about it than Trip did. But perfect or not, Mr. Something-Something Hedgeclipper the Fourteenth was in for a surprise. DiDi can be all sugar sweet and everything, but unless Trip convinced her he was my new math tutor, I probably wasn't going anywhere.

"Hi, Miss Clarisse," I said as we walked in.

"Good afternoon, GiGi, and a good afternoon to you, Mr. Trip! What a wonderful surprise! Are you meeting your mother here today? I didn't see her name in the appointment book!"

"I just came to introduce myself to G's sister."

"Well, aren't you the perfect gentleman."

Trip glanced at me, like *I told you so.*

"DiDi is with a client, but go on back. You know where the cookies and treats are!"

We got to DiDi's station just in time to see her do this really snazzy thing where she takes the haircutting cape and kind of whips it up in the air all swoopy and dramatic before she puts it on her customer. I was thinking about saying something like how Trip better watch out for DiDi and her attack cape, when suddenly, everything just kind of went into slow motion.

DiDi has always been big into TV shows. Even cartoons with superheroes and such. When I was little, she would say stuff like "You gotta watch this, Double G!" But even as a little kid, I wasn't much for silliness and imagination and I'd say "There's no such thing as superheroes, DiDi."

But as I watched that cape fly around Mace's smug face, I couldn't help thinking that in a world where there was no such thing as superheroes, she sure made one heck of an evil supervillain.

Madder'n Heck Smashed Potatoes

- 1 pound new baby potatoes
- 1 tablespoon vegetable oil
- 1 tablespoon butter
- Salt and pepper
- Sour cream

Get the littlest, darn cutest new potatoes you can find and scrub the heck out of those babies until they gleam like little moons.

Dump 'em in a big old pot filled with cold water and a couple of shakes of salt and then set it to boil.

Lower the heat to a simmer and cook until the potatoes are fork tender. Maybe about 20 minutes, depending on how big they are, but please check them, because you don't want them to turn to mush. Scoop 'em out real careful and dry them off with a kitchen towel. Now let them sit and relax a bit.

Turn the heat under your skillet to medium high and put in the oil and butter. Put a few potatoes in there. Just enough so they have some room to spread. Here's the fun part. Take a big clean can of beans (please make sure you've washed and dried it because I do not know what has been scampering around your pantry!) and smash down on each potato till it's like a chubby pancake.

Fry 'em on each side till they're golden brown. You get a crispy cracklin' outside and a soft fluffy inside. Add lots of salt and pepper, and you know, if you're all that mad, you're going to need a heck of a lot of sour cream.

Now sit yourself down, eat 'em all up, and wonder what you were so mad about in the first place.

Serves 1 (unless you have a friend who's just as mad and doesn't mind sharing).

sixteen

Now, I'm not one for cursing, but when I saw that smug look on Mace's face, I was madder'n heck. She was going to do something to make DiDi and me look bad in front of Trip. It didn't matter how I'd folded my way into his buttery, sugary group. Mace was going to make me look like the sardine someone had decided to throw into her perfect recipe. I mumbled something about the ladies' room and ran in as quickly as I could.

I splashed my face with icy, icy water and stared into the mirror. And laughed. It didn't even matter if Mace ruined things with Trip, because DiDi would Get Grammatical the second I told her I wanted to hang out with a boy after school anyway. Nothing was going to go right no matter what I did. So there was only one thing to do: Get my Recipe for Success face on and be the smart, classy girl that my mama would be if she were here.

When I walked out, DiDi was holding the pretty box with the cookie in it. I guess Trip said something and used those Wish Pie eyes on her, because next thing you know, she was giving him a big hug. She pushed the hair out of his face.

"You are one beautiful boy, sweetheart. Isn't he, Double G?"

Geez, DiDi. I could feel my cheeks blaze. Even though I had the exact same thought the first time I saw him, it was just plain mortifying to hear DiDi say it out loud. Trip was turning a little red himself.

"Double G?" Mace looked back and forth between DiDi and me. "What's Double G?"

DiDi winked. "Just an inside joke, honey. Don't you worry about it."

"Do you like the cookie?" I burst out to change the subject. "Trip got me one, too."

"Well, it's just too pretty to eat. What a gentleman you are."

Mace cleared her throat. "Can we get back to me, please? As you can probably tell, my mom and I are very particular about my hair."

"DiDi said it was cool for you to come over for dinner." Trip grinned at me.

"Really?"

"Sure," DiDi said. "Just give me till closing time, and I'll rev up the Blue Bomb."

"My mom is playing tennis at our club. It's like a fifteen-minute walk from here and she can drive us. Is it okay if we hang out and watch a movie, too? It's Friday and we don't have any homework, and I know my mom wouldn't mind driving G back. She just got a new car and she wants to drive it all the time."

Hold on now.

It was Friday night.

And Trip was asking me to hang out with him. For dinner and a movie.

Was this a date? Was I allowed to date?

According to DiDi's schedule, I wasn't supposed to date until I had a PhD in Ruling the Universe.

Mace cleared her throat again. "Usually, my mom will only let Jean touch my hair. After all, he's the best. You know he trained in Paris—did you?"

DiDi waved us on. "Why don't you run along, then, and let me take care of Macy here. Just call me if anything changes. Now, Mace, honey, Jean is a genius, but if you ask me..."

"Let's get out of here," I said to Trip. "See you, D."

"It was really great meeting you, DiDi," said Trip. "Um, bye...Mace."

I looked back. Mace's chin was still up, but she didn't look like an evil villain in a dark cape anymore. She looked more like a little girl. In a big blanket. Being left behind.

seventeen

"See?" Trip said when we got outside. "Grown-ups love me." He pointed to himself. "Perfect Boy."

"Oh, please. She's just tired from a hard day's work. She's delirious from the hair spray fumes. She's dazzled by that crazy cookie, wrapped up like Christmas morning. She never lets me out of her sight."

"But seriously, you're lucky you have a sister like DiDi," he said. "I don't have anyone."

"DiDi?" I thought about her. She was just, well, DiDi. "The thing is..."

"What?" Trip said. "What are you thinking?"

Do people really ask that? DiDi never asks about feelings

that much. We're just always so busy trying to figure out my next steps.

"It's just that…" I looked at the ground. Then up into Trip's eyes. "DiDi never even finished school. She had to drop out and work. And even before that, it's not like she was the—the smartest. I guess I'm lucky because if I didn't have DiDi, I'd be all alone, but we're just so different. She has all these yakkity ideas, and there's just so much she doesn't know and…and that's what I'm thinking."

We walked along quietly for a bit.

"Was that…weird to tell me all that personal stuff about your sister?"

I thought about it. Then I told him the truth.

"No. But only because it never feels weird telling you anything."

Trip looked at me for a long time and then nodded.

eighteen

The Harbor Club was the country club that Trip and his family belonged to.

Trip had belonged his whole life.

His daddy had belonged his whole life.

His granddaddy had belonged his whole life.

And so on and so on—all the way back to the very first Something-Something Hedgeclipper caveman, I guess. I was a little nervous walking in. I'd never been in any kind of country club before.

"Are we allowed to come in with our school uniforms?" I whispered.

"Of course," Trip said. But I noticed that his tie wasn't rumply anymore and his shirt was tucked in. "I don't see my mom anywhere yet. Do you want to sit and have a soda or something?"

"Um." I couldn't imagine how much money a soda would cost in a place like this, and I felt bad if Trip was going to keep treating me all the time. "Maybe just water. Thanks."

We walked into this nice patio area. He ordered us these drinks that were half iced tea and half lemonade. A lot like sweet tea back home, but a little more tart. They were cold and delicious and had really pretty lemon slices and mint stuck in them. I could just imagine DiDi slicing the lemons and smiling while she balanced them on the edge of a glass for her imaginary cooking show.

Then Trip started talking.

About growing up in this town.

How it felt like everyone was the same.

How he couldn't wait to finish middle school. And high school. And go somewhere for college that was far, far away. And big. And different. But he was scared of that, too.

When he was done, he looked up and pushed the hair out of his face. "Sorry. I didn't mean to—"

"No—no—it's fine." I could hardly breathe. I didn't want anything to break the spell. "Trip, you can tell me any—"

"Mom!" Trip jumped up and kissed a tall woman in a white tennis dress. "Mom, hi. This is G—I mean, I'd like you to meet my friend Leia Barnes."

Trip's mom put a cool hand in mine. "Hello, Leia, how

nice to meet you." She was probably the prettiest grown-up lady I'd ever seen in my life.

I forced myself to smile big, wishing Trip and I could have kept talking and talking. "Hi, Mrs. Davis, it's really nice to meet you, too. Thank you for having me to your house."

"Oh, it's our pleasure."

"Trip and, well, just everybody has been so extra welcoming since we moved here."

"From the South, I assume. Your accent is charming. Where exactly did you move from?"

For some reason, the way Trip suddenly stopped looking at me and started playing with the tablecloth was making alarms go off in my head. But I wasn't sure why. Maybe I didn't have to talk about the trailer park or Say It Like It Is about everything. "Um, South Carolina, ma'am. But we love it here and I am just thankful and happy we moved."

Then Trip smiled.

His mom smiled, too.

But I had a feeling she was going to wait and decide about me later.

Nineteen

Trip's mom's car sure was clean. I know that sounds like a funny thing to say, but it really was the first thing I noticed. I didn't even want to put my backpack on the seat next to me.

"Your car is so pretty," I said to Mrs. Davis, remembering how Trip said it was new.

"Thank you," she said, looking toward Trip. "It's nice to know there is a young person around here who appreciates it. We've told Trip we'd order one for him when he turns sixteen, but he and Billy have it in their heads that they're going to get Billy's dad to part with a couple of his prize convertibles."

"Mom," Trip said. "C'mon, stop." He looked all embarrassed.

I wasn't quite sure what to say. "Well, any of those would

be better than our car. It's, like, fifty years old and you have to give the door a real kick to open it. We call it the Blue Bomb."

"Oh my," said Mrs. Davis. "How colorful."

Trip's house was a few miles from town along these winding roads by the water. I guess I just figured it was going to be a crazy huge mansion like all the other homes in the neighborhood.

But it was this really beautiful cottage. White, with windows everywhere and tucked behind a rise in the hill like it was hiding from the world. From the porch, there was a view of the water. I stood there and felt the wind on my face, thinking if I had this view, I'd have all the windows wide open all day, every day—not shut tight to the world with fancy curtains. I thought about our apartment with the view of the candy store on Main Street that I had been so excited about. I wondered what Trip's mom would think of it.

Trip's dad was just getting home when we got there. We had stopped at this Chinese restaurant to pick up dinner. I had never known that ordering food was such a big deal, but Trip's mom sure had a lot to say on the matter:

"Would you prefer Szechuan or Cantonese, Leia?"

"It won't be nearly as good as Chinatown, but it will have to do."

"They claim to be authentic, but look at this menu—though I guess most people wouldn't know. . . ."

I wasn't sure exactly how to answer, so I just nodded. "DiDi always says if you took all the things most people don't know, you could fill the Grand Canyon."

The dining table in their house had this sparkly crystal chandelier over it with all these drops hanging down, and Mrs. Davis set the table really formal even though I was the only guest. And I just have to say that everything on that table was *B, I, G,* BIG. These humongous plates and napkins and everything. It was like she went shopping at the Giant Supply Store. She even put the food onto huge serving platters with big silver serving spoons instead of just having everyone dig into the white cartons like I thought we would.

"Does your mom cook at home?" Mrs. Davis asked.

Before I could open my mouth, Trip answered, "Leia's mom and dad died when she was a baby, Mom. She lives with her big sister, DiDi."

I looked at Trip, thinking about how he sort of stuck my daddy in there even though I'd told him that I'd never even met my daddy, let alone had a clue about who he was. Being brainy works a couple of different ways. I said before about how I'm good at math, but I'm also good at adding stuff up that has nothing to do with math. Well, what I was adding up was that maybe Trip's parents didn't need to know my whole history and family tree in the first hour of meeting me. I wondered if Trip felt like I had told him too much. But then I remembered how he was always telling me he liked how open I was. It was confusing.

"I'm so sorry to hear that," said Mrs. Davis. "How do you manage? How old is your sister?"

She was probably thinking about the tuition. At that moment I didn't know what to talk about. I sure didn't think I should bring up the coupon clipping. Or waiting till milk went on sale even though we were millionaires.

"Well…we're nine years, nine days, and nine hours apart," I said. "DiDi says it's like this lucky voodoo thing. So I'll be thirteen on November twentieth and nine days later, she'll be twenty-two on the twenty-ninth."

"How charming," Trip's mother said.

"Lucky voodoo. I like it," Trip's dad said.

I was watching Trip and trying to figure out what else I wasn't supposed to talk about when I remembered something that might be interesting. "Oh, and speaking of birthdays, the Founder's Day Gala is right before mine, and DiDi is in charge of the whole menu. So it'll practically be like having the biggest birthday party ever."

Trip's mom put down the giant glass of wine she had just picked up.

"Your sister is the one who is doing the Gala?" She was looking at me with that same studying look that Trip had. "Yes, I remember her from Welcome Night." She picked up her chopsticks and popped a snow pea into her mouth. Then smiled as she chewed.

"DiDi is really nice," Trip said. "I met her at Jean René's."

"Oh, how lovely. Was she getting her hair done?"

"No," I said, trying to stab a slippery piece of chicken with my fork. I was the only one not using chopsticks. "She's the new hairdresser there. She's really, really good, too."

Trip's dad winked. "Well, if she's as pretty as you, I'm heading straight there tomorrow for a haircut."

Mrs. Davis smiled and continued chewing.

After dinner, Trip showed me his room. It was locked, but he pulled out the key from this chain around his neck. Before we went in, he took this deep breath and then opened the door.

"What do you think?"

I looked around. He had this huge desk and shelves just spilling over with books. About everything. One wall was completely covered in cork and had about a million photos pinned to it. Camp photos. Sports photos. School photos. Laughing, smiling photos. Friends. Friends. Friends.

"I just love it," I said.

He nodded toward his pictures. "Do you miss all your friends back home?"

"Not—exactly," I said. "I've always been really busy. Studying. So I never had a ton of friends or anything." I turned back to the photos. "I just—I really—" I didn't know how to end the sentence. "Well, to be honest, if you hadn't asked me over, I guess I'd be home studying now."

"I don't have a ton of friends, either...." Trip began.

"Oh, please," I said, waving at the pictures. "You know everyone."

"Okay. A lot of people know me, but having people know you isn't the same as...people really...knowing you." He looked at his feet. "I'm glad you're...it's nice to have someone to..."

What?

Hold hands with in front of Mace?

"...to talk to and be myself with."

I looked at him. "You're not yourself?"

"I am. It's just..." He stopped, then went to his desk. I heard him scribbling and then folding paper. When he turned back around, he had a KOB in his hand.

Wait till you get home to read.

I took it and nodded.

After ice cream and popcorn and a zombie movie (I covered my eyes the whole time while Trip tried to convince me to watch), we figured it was time for me to head home. It was getting pretty late, and there was no way DiDi would stand for that, no matter how much Trip used his Wish Pie eyes on her.

We were getting ready to leave when the phone rang.

Trip and I waited in this big hallway filled with fancy wooden cubbies and shelves and coat hooks and a row of matching navy rain boots. He called it the Mudroom, but I can guarantee there was not one speck of mud in there.

We overheard Trip's mom talking on the phone. "Calm down, Tish. Talk to me. Who do you want to have fired? Go back and talk to Jean. What does it look like? It can't be as bad as—oh dear..."

Trip looked at me.

"What is it?" I asked.

"Tish is Mace's mom," he whispered.

The bottom of my stomach dropped faster than if I'd just eaten a triple-decker cannonball sandwich.

What had DiDi done to Mace's hair?

twenty

Mrs. Davis didn't say a word on the drive home except for "It was lovely to meet you, Leia. I hope you have a nice year at school." Like she didn't expect me to be around much. Or at least around her son much.

I nodded at her and stared at Trip for a minute, then ran out the door and up the stairs to our apartment. I was fumbling for my keys but just couldn't dig them out of my backpack. What had DiDi done? What would school be like on Monday with frizzy-headed Mace leading the crowds against me? And would Trip still stand by me?

The door across the hall flew open and Kenneth stuck his head out. "Uh—oh, hi, GiGi."

"It's Leia, Kenneth," I said, still fumbling with my keys.

"Oh, uh, how are you?"

"Fine, Kenneth."

"Would you, uh, say hi to DiDi and—and tell her if she ever, uh, needs help around the place, I'm, uh, pretty handy. They have me fixing the lights over at the library."

I dropped my keys in frustration. Great. The one time Kenneth decided to loosen up and yak, it was now.

"Hold on, I got it!" I heard DiDi call from inside. Two clicks and a clunk and the door opened. "I swear, girl, where do you keep your keys? It sounded like you were unpacking from a week's vacation out there. Come on in. You're just in time. I'm working on ideas for the Gala menu. Hi, Kenneth. Bye, Kenneth." She pulled me in and shut the door.

When I walked in, it didn't look like DiDi had been working on the Gala at all. Mama's Cookbook was nowhere in sight, and she had that darn cooking show on again. With the Mystery Basket. I don't even know why DiDi watches it. Like she's going to make anything that's not written in stone in Mama's Cookbook.

DiDi strolled back to the sofa and plopped down. "Oh, by the way. Your teacher, Mr. McSomethin'?"

"McGuire."

"That's the one. He called and left a message about a meeting after school next week."

"Fine."

Then I just stood there, ticking like a stopwatch that

127

might explode if someone didn't get me what I needed in the next ninety seconds. You better make that ten seconds.

"What? Oh yeah. How was your evening? Cute boy, that Trip," she said. "Cute, cute, cute." She was smiling and smiling, because there's nothing good-looking people love better than other good-looking people.

When I didn't answer, DiDi shrugged. "Fine, girl, don't tell me if you don't want. Do you want to sit a few minutes and talk about the Gala and—what?"

"What did you do?" I said through shut teeth.

"What did I do when?"

"What did you do to Mace's hair?"

"Oh! Did she call you up and tell you? What do you think?"

I began to shout. "No, she did not call me up and tell me—why? Because I am the only millionaire in this town without a cell phone—not to mention she hates me! Geez, DiDi, don't you ever listen to a word I say? How many Chinese girls do you think there are in this school who hate me? I told you about her! The only reason she went to Jean's was to pick on you! And now you've gone and ruined her hair, and her mom is going to get you fired, and she is going to make my life miserable—all because of you! Why can't you be a normal person and play tennis? Why do you have to be a hairdresser?"

My chest was heaving. I couldn't breathe. I don't think I've ever shouted at DiDi like that in my life.

"What in the world are you—"

"And what about food?"

"What—what in heck are you talking about? What about food?"

"Why don't we ever get Chinese takeout? Why do we have to eat these same stupid meals every day of the week? Stupid fake food trying to be something it's not! Why is it everything we eat is trying to be something else? Why can't one thing in my life be real?"

"You wait one minute, Double G—"

"I WANT TO BE CALLED LEIA!"

There was a second of silence.

DiDi's eyes narrowed and her voice went low. "You better listen here, Little Miss Whatever Your Pants Are. Don't you ever talk to me in that tone of voice. I don't know what you think, but I do have a normal job. And what do you mean I'm getting fired? That girl, Mace, loved what I did! As a matter of fact, we spent about an hour just talking about it, and it was all her idea and I thought it was brilliant. Maybe if you spent a little time getting to know her instead of worrying about her hating you, you'd feel different."

"You—you spent an hour with—?"

"And on top of that, G, I cook a homemade meal for you three times a day, every day, seven days a week, all year long. Enough said. Just—just go brush your teeth and go to bed." She sat back down with her arms crossed. "I don't think I can stand to look at you anymore tonight."

I ran into my room, tears blinding me.

What had just happened? DiDi wasn't fired. Mace was happy. But Trip and I had heard that phone conversation, and it did not sound like anyone was happy. And what was all this about DiDi spending an hour talking to Mace about hair? DiDi listened to what Mace wanted? DiDi never had that kind of time for me—but she did for Mace? I wished I were back in Trip's room, talking to him and looking into his Wish Pie eyes.

Trip! I yanked the KOB out of my pocket. *Wait till you get home to read.*

I opened it.

> *The Truth is I feel like I can be more myself with you than with anyone. T*

I held the note close to me, then carefully folded it back up and put it under my pillow. Who needed DiDi? I decided not to brush my teeth and just throw myself into bed to teach her a lesson. How dare she yell at me? I had never had a cavity in my life! Why was she telling me to brush my teeth? Maybe I'd just skip it tonight and get my first cavity, and she'd have to pay for it out of that precious million dollars that I was not even allowed to have a look at.

But after lying there for a minute, I got up and brushed them anyway. We'd had a lot of popcorn and sticky stuff at Trip's house. And it only takes one night of plaque buildup to cause damage to your tooth enamel.

twenty-one

The rest of the weekend was like a stopwatch that wouldn't stop ticking.

DiDi and I barely spoke. On Saturday, she began mentioning that we were supposed to work on the Gala ideas, but I quickly grabbed my backpack and headed for the door, mumbling I was doing extra volunteering at the library.

The next day at home, I stayed in my room and buried myself in my books. I studied. I studied. And I studied. Mostly, I studied the paint on the walls that was peeling like a summer's sunburn, but DiDi didn't have to know that.

Monday at school, I think I was more nervous than the first day.

Even though The Honeycomb was filled with people

bustling around, bumping into each other, busy getting where they needed to go, I felt like I was alone. Walking down one of those big empty hallways like you have in a dream. Trip ran up beside me.

I grabbed his arm. "What did your mom say? Did she tell you what happened?"

He shook his head.

"Well, I guess I'll see you in English class." I didn't mention that we'd see Mace there, too. "I have to stop at my locker first. Will you wait for me outside the door?"

"Okay," he said. "DiDi won't get fired. Don't be scared."

I didn't bother telling him that, except for those zombie movies he loves, I've just never been the type to be scared. Of anything. There used to be a story about Dead Drunk Donna and the long-suffering manager of the trailer park where she lived and how he was scared out of his skull on Package Day. There weren't a lot of people getting special deliveries to that trailer park—except for her—and the box was always the same. Plainly wrapped in brown paper and not much to look at. Now, that manager admitted he didn't know a lot about guns and ammo and such, but it only took one peek through her window for him to learn fast. And why Dead Drunk Donna was getting a regular supply of golden bullets delivered to her, no one knew or wanted to guess. But they say that poor man shook like a baby when he had to walk past the dead bear tied to her tree, knock on her door, and have her sign for that box.

On the way to class, I heard Mace's name murmured here and there down the hallways. I tried to close my ears so I wouldn't have to hear more, and just kept looking out for Trip. He'd said he'd meet me outside the door, but as I walked toward it, I could see he wasn't there.

I figured he had probably done the math and realized that being friends with the sister of the hairdresser who messed up Mace's hair was probably not doing him any good. I started thinking about what it would be like to find a table by myself at lunch and get extra-credit work done. I still had perfect grades. But that didn't mean I couldn't just focus on working harder. Maybe I could skip a grade. Or three. Graduate a few years early. Move out of town. Maybe even out of the country. Or off the planet.

It was still early and Mr. McGuire hadn't settled everyone down yet. I quickly looked around for Trip. I spotted him in the back row talking and—my heart did a little bumpity-bump—my seat was still free and waiting for me. Maybe it would be okay. I started rushing toward him.

Then froze.

The person talking to Trip.

Was Mace.

Laughing and swinging her hair all around. It was short

and choppy, higher on one side than the other, with long swishy bangs and all these cute little pieces pointing around her face. A single streak of icy blue fell across one cheek. She looked like a rock star.

We locked eyes a second; then Mace looked away.

Trip was talking on and on like it was all a big joke. It was practically the most I'd ever seen him speak. To anyone. "...And then, my mom is on the phone with yours and her voice starts doing—you know, the—"

"Not the Squirrel!"

"Yes—it was just like that time with the tomatoes—"

"Which was so your idea, by the way!"

"It was not!"

"But you started the other thing—"

"What thing?"

"The Thing."

"*You* did—"

"Actually, yeah. That was me—and it was awesome!" They were leaning away from me, and laughing and laughing.

Trip watched her for a second, then looked down, and his smile faded. His hair fell over his eyes and his voice went low and mumbly. "I'm sorry ab—"

Mace's smile faded, too. "It's okay."

"It was stupid—"

"Forget it."

I looked back and forth between them. What was happening?

"Cool." Billy was standing there. "Does this mean we can start having playdates in the Cave again?"

Mace laughed. "Ha! You wish. You so got kicked out."

"C'mon, I was, like, six. Your mom can't still be mad. The smell's gotta be gone by now."

Mace and Trip looked at each other and burst out laughing again.

I just stood there, staring. Trip and Mace bonding about tomatoes and squirrels and a cave? They probably had a whole life of memories and jokes together I didn't know about. I thought about the photos on Trip's wall. How many were Mace in? I knew how many had me. Big fat zero.

Mr. McGuire was clearing his throat and trying to get everyone quiet.

"Miss Galileo, if you could take your seat, you can start us off by saying something Truthful about yourself—nothing too personal, now. No confessions. Just one small thing. Something to spark your Truth-in-poetry assignment. For example, I'll start: My vinyl record problem—ahem—*collection* is now up to a staggering eighty-one albums."

I turned and looked at him blankly.

All I could think about was this salad DiDi used to make for potluck dinners. It's covered with this blanket of mayonnaise on top, so you assume it's all bland and mayo through and through. What you don't see is that right under that blanket of bland, there's all this stuff just hiding there. Waiting. Waiting for someone to realize there's more to it than just mayo. I used to feel sorry for that salad whenever I saw it sitting there on the table with no one digging in. But now I think it was lying in wait. All mayo and innocence on the outside, not letting us know what it really was on the inside.

"Miss Galileo?"

I looked up at Mr. McGuire. The Truth?

"May I be excused? I—I think I just lost something."

Secret Layered Salad

Salad

- 1 head of iceberg lettuce, chopped
- Salt and pepper to taste
- 8 hard-boiled eggs, chopped
- 1 pound bacon, cooked and chopped
- 4 whole tomatoes, chopped
- 1 cup of carrots, thinly sliced
- 1 bunch of green onions, thinly sliced
- 2 cups cheddar cheese, grated
- 1 bag (14 ounces) of frozen sweet peas, partially thawed

Dressing

- ½ cup real mayonnaise
- ½ cup sour cream
- 1 tablespoon lemon juice

Now, I'll just tell you that this was not always called Secret Layered Salad. It used to be just good old Layered Salad because I always made it in my favorite glass bowl so you could see all the pretty layers. Then Mary Elizabeth Clark broke it during a potluck last summer. Yes, I wrote your name right here plain as day, Mary Elizabeth, so don't you dare scratch it out next time you borrow this! Anyway, I just started using my big white Pyrex bowl.

Start with half the iceberg lettuce and then add the rest of the ingredients in the order listed, adding salt and pepper to each layer, till the bowl is full. Top with the rest of the lettuce. Mix the mayo, sour cream, and lemon juice in another bowl, and cover the whole salad, sealing it around the edges. It may look like a whole lot of nothing, but it's delicious!

And so what if you can't see the layers anymore? I say the most interesting things have more to them than just what you see on the outside. And that's a fact.

Serves 12–14 as a side salad at a potluck.

twenty-two

That day at lunch, everyone was surrounding Mace and telling her how awesome her hair looked. I just sat there, looking at my PB&B&B sandwich. Not able to eat anything.

"Are you okay?" Trip whispered.

I tried a weak smile. "Yeah, just, um, a tummyache."

Mace stopped in the middle of whatever story she was telling and looked right at me. "You probably need to go to the nurse. C'mon, I'll walk you."

Billy looked up at Mace offering to walk me anywhere and then shook his head. "Girls, man."

Trip was watching me quietly.

Mace stood up. "Well? Are you coming?" It was almost like a challenge.

"Maybe..." I said. "Yeah, I'll go."

I stood up, leaving my lunch, which Billy pounced on. "Yes! Peanut butter, banana, and bacon on white! Sweet!"

Mace said nothing as the two of us walked out of the cafeteria. She paused in front of Miss Homer, who was hidden behind her latest book, and said, "Leia doesn't feel well. I'm just going to walk her to the nurse."

"Mmm-hmm." Page turn.

It was touching how concerned she was for my welfare.

We said nothing in the quiet halls. Just walked and listened to the soft echo of our steps.

Right outside the health office, Mace paused and said, "Look, I still don't like you—and I don't care if you like me or not, but—"

I just stood there. Was this why she wanted to walk me? So she could tell me how much she still didn't like me? I kept my mouth shut and waited. Whatever she was handing out, I could take.

"But I—I really like DiDi. Having someone listen and talk to me...it means everything to me."

It was like being on another planet.

Mace was standing there, saying she liked DiDi.

That DiDi meant everything to her.

My DiDi.

My DiDi, who was born nine years, nine days, and nine hours apart from me. And Mace had known her for how

140

long? Nine seconds? I could feel the angry part of me growing and growing. And then I opened my mouth and let it do the talking.

"Well—you mean nothing to her—do you hear me? Nothing. She doesn't even like you—she could never like someone as—as fussy—and stuck-up as you. She did that to your hair as a joke."

Then I opened the nurse's door and slammed it as hard as I could, leaving her standing there, looking like I'd just punched her in the face.

One-Two Punch

- Two quarts orange sherbet
- Two liters ginger ale
- One large can of pineapple juice (46 ounces)
- 1 lemon and 1 orange, sliced in circles, for garnish

When you're ready to get this party started, just put your orange sherbet in your best punch bowl.

Pour in your ginger ale. Then your pineapple juice.

Top it with some lemon and orange slices to make it pretty.

Couldn't be easier.

But then, I always say, it doesn't take much to make the perfect One-Two Punch.

Serves a whole party of people.

twenty-three

The next few days, I tried to act like everything was the same. But it wasn't.

Mace didn't give me those glaring looks anymore. She pretty much pretended I wasn't there at all. But she looked at Trip a lot. He sure seemed happy to have her there. And I hadn't gotten a KOB since the night at Trip's house.

I found myself walking with Billy after English and watching them walk ahead.

"So, Trip and Mace have known each other since they were little?" I tried to sound casual.

"Yeah, their moms were in the same sorority in college, and they're neighbors now." He laughed. "Man, she has the most awesome house. It looks like a fort and it has this secret bomb shelter in it. Like this cool cave. We all used to play there when we were kids. Trust me, if there's ever an earthquake, go there."

My chest was starting to hurt.

"Hey, are you coming to the last big soccer game on Saturday? Trip's family is doing a tailgate."

I thought quickly. "Um, I wish I could, but I . . . oh, I have the Stargazers and—we have this big meeting."

"Big meeting with the three of you?"

I glared at him.

"Okay—just kidding. But you should come. Bring the science girls when you're done figuring out how to rule the universe."

"Okay," I said. "Thanks, I'll try."

But I knew I wouldn't.

I called Haven and Allie right after school and invited them over for the morning of the soccer game and tailgate to make sure I was busy that day. "To plan our conquest of the stars!" I shouted, acting all enthusiastic. But truth is I wasn't up for conquering anything, except this terrible feeling in my heart.

Haven and Allie both seemed so excited that it just really made me wish I'd done it sooner.

Saturday morning, DiDi was up bright and early, making Mama's Special-Occasion Fancy Tea Sandwiches. I thought it was kind of much for just having friends over, but I didn't say a word. It had been pretty quiet between me and DiDi since the fight over Mace's hair. I never brought it up again and neither did she. I guess we don't have a lot of experience fighting, so we don't have a lot of experience making up, either.

When the doorbell buzzed, I let Allie and Haven in. They kind of paused and that made me think they were probably used to being in houses like Trip's or Mace's. Not old one-bedroom apartments with DiDi's sheets and blankets still folded on the side of the pull-out sofa bed. I ran over and quickly picked them up and folded the sofa bed back into place. Then for the first time, I thought about how DiDi let me have the one bedroom.

"Hey, come on in."

Allie and Haven walked in carrying several notebooks and two huge tote bags filled with what looked like craft-making supplies.

"Um, this is my sister, DiDi. DiDi, this is Allie and that's Haven."

"Hi, girls. Nice to meet you. We are going to have so much fun today!"

I looked back and forth between DiDi in the kitchen and the girls standing in the living room. "Uh, D, what do you mean *we*? Did you want to help us with Stargazers?"

DiDi stopped cutting the crusts off sandwiches and looked up. "Didn't you ask the girls to come with us to the tailgate? With, you know, Trip and Mace and their families? Mace mentioned it yesterday when we were talking—"

"You talked to Mace?" I said. "When? Why? How?"

DiDi raised an eyebrow. "Now who's Getting Grammatical? Calm down, honey, she just calls me sometimes for girl talk. I know you two had a rough start, but you should give her a chance. She's a regular human girl just like you. C'mon, we'll all go and it'll be fun." DiDi smiled at Allie and Haven, who still looked puzzled.

"I thought we were having a Stargazers meeting, but…" Allie glanced over at the big basket that DiDi was preparing and then looked at Haven.

Haven hesitated. "It's just that we don't—we don't really hang out with those guys—"

"Oh pooh!" said DiDi. "You'll be hanging with us—we'll take care of you, won't we, Double G?"

"NO!" The sound of my voice surprised even me. "And I'm NOT Grammatical!" Allie and Haven were staring. "This meeting is really important—I want to plan a trip to the observatory here, because I've never seen the one that this town has and—"

"Double G, calm down. What are you going on about? What do you think I've been doing? I made a whole mess of fancy tea sandwiches, and all I have to do is take a quick shower and I'll be all set to head to the game. I thought you'd want to go. And it looks like these girls do."

The girls looked interested, but you could tell they were concerned about my feelings.

"It could be fun," Allie said. "But..." She glanced at Haven.

"But we don't have to—if Leia doesn't want to..." Haven said.

"Listen, Double G, why don't you girls talk your science stuff while I shower up? My sweet tea needs a little more time to chill anyway."

"What's Double G?" asked Allie.

"Fine. I don't care. You decide." I threw myself on the sofa.

"Great!" DiDi popped into the bathroom and then stuck her head out. "Does anyone have to, you know, *go* before I shower? Sorry, girls, but this is a one-stop pit stop—if you know what I mean."

I squirmed. I was pretty sure that Allie and Haven each had private baths they didn't have to share with anyone. Not to mention separate guest quarters for any guests lucky enough to have to pee at their house.

"Last chance!" DiDi winked and then clicked the door shut.

We heard the shower start.

"What's Double G?" Allie asked again.

Haven put a hand on my arm. "Did you and Trip break up?"

"Is he going out with Mace now?" Allie said.

I pulled away. Then regretted it. "No. We're just friends and Mace is just a friend. I mean, they've known each other since they were little and . . . and . . ."

Haven reached out and patted my arm. And I started to think that even if she didn't know how I felt, maybe she really wanted to.

"Do you—do you still want to make some plans for Stargazers while we're waiting for DiDi?" she said.

I nodded. I didn't know what else to do. I tried my best to sound involved in everything the girls were saying, but truth is I didn't hear a word. Which was just as well, because after a few minutes, Allie and Haven gave up and started talking about other things.

"Will your mom bring back goodies from the conference?" Allie asked.

"Yes!" said Haven. "I'll bring you a goody bag. Do you want a goody bag, too, Leia?"

I came out of my fog. "Goody who?"

"Goody bag. My mom is at this huge conference, looking at all the new colors coming out next year. You know, for the city store? She's always bringing back loads of awesome new stuff. But some of it's gross, too—Al, do you remember when she brought all that purple-y lipstick home last year? Ew!" She and Allie screamed.

"Lipstick," I said.

"It totally made you look like you'd been eating dirt, Leia. It was the worst."

Allie sighed. "I hope this year is more a sparkly pink year."

"Yeah, or I don't mind purple—just more for nail polish than lips."

I looked at the two of them, happy and chatting away.

I pictured DiDi happily listening to Mace talk on the phone all night.

Then I took a breath.

"Does your mom—would your mom know if a company decided to bring back an old lipstick?"

Allie made a face. "Old?"

"Like colors they don't make anymore."

Haven shrugged. "I'll ask. I remember this one time there was a color that they brought back for, like, an anniversary or something. There were signs all over the place."

Allie looked at me. "Is there a lipstick you can't live without, Leia? You don't seem like the makeup-y type."

"No...I just had this idea...." I glanced at the bathroom door and lowered my voice. "For a special birthday gift for DiDi...a surprise."

The girls looked excited.

"Tell us!" Haven whispered. "Let us help!"

"Really?" I said.

"Yes! What can we do?" Allie was jumping up and down.

I guessed this was what it was like to have girlfriends. So I put away my agenda for the Stargazers. The girls and I huddled together on our old sofa, and I told them about Mama and Cherries in the Snow.

You know, it's funny how you never really know how special any occasion is going to be till you're in the middle of it. Like, in all honesty, I had really only invited Haven and Allie over so I'd have an excuse not to go to that stupid tailgate with Trip and his future rock star girlfriend, Mace. And here, for the first time ever, I was talking to someone other than DiDi about Mama's lipstick.

And for the first time, I started thinking that maybe—just maybe—impossible wishes really did sometimes become... possible.

If you ask me, that's pretty special.

Special-Occasion Fancy Tea Sandwiches

I say no occasion is special until you personally put a little effort into it.

Now, my mama was a real Southern Lady and knew how to do a nice afternoon tea.

First of all, make sure you use only thinly sliced white bread with the crusts cut off. (I save the crusts in a plastic bag in the freezer for stuffing.) The recipes here are enough for two people to have two pieces of each sandwich. Double as necessary.

Cucumber Sandwiches

- Mayonnaise
- Cucumbers, thinly sliced
- Salt and pepper
- Parsley, chopped fine

Spread each slice of your sandwich bread with the thinnest bit of mayonnaise you can spread. Pile 8 to 10 slices of cucumber on one side. Salt and pepper. Top with the other slice of bread. Trim off any cucumber sticking out over the edges. Then cut the sandwich into 4 triangles. Spread very thin mayo on one edge of each of the triangles and then dip that into your chopped parsley. Arrange on a plate, standing up like little sails with the parsley side showing.

Pepper Jelly Triple-Decker Surprise Sandwiches

- Pepper jelly
- Cream cheese

Spread pepper jelly on one slice of bread and cream cheese on the other. You know what to do—put them together. Now spread cream cheese on the top of that sandwich. Take another slice of bread and spread pepper jelly on that and put it on top. You should now have a triple-decker sandwich with pretty stripes. These get sliced into 4 long fingers.

Pimento Cheese and Tomato Sandwiches

• Pimento cheese (I know I put my pimento cheese recipe in here somewhere. Just look it up because I am not writing it down again.)
• Cherry tomatoes

This is a real pretty open-face sandwich. Spread your pimento cheese on a slice of bread all the way to the edges. Cut the bread into quarters. Slice 2 cherry tomatoes in half. Top each bread quarter with a tomato half, cut side up.

If you have a wait before you start eating, cover the sandwiches with a wet paper towel that you've wrung out till it's just damp. I like to arrange them all nice and fancy on my pressed-glass plate that I got from my mama. Then I call a girlfriend over for a chat and some sweet tea. What occasion could be more special than that?

Serves 2.

twenty-four

When DiDi was finally all showered up and squeaky clean and had her hair pulled back so tight not one curl could even think about getting out, we headed down to the street, where our car was parked.

You can probably guess that I was just about thrilled at the idea of Mace, Trip, and all the parents at the soccer game getting a look at the Blue Bomb. Like I said before, I figured with a million dollars, it was time for an upgrade, and it wasn't like I was asking for a solid-gold limo with a diamond steering wheel.

Back home, Lori had this really cute little car that I loved. She called it The Bug. It was bright yellow, and whenever we needed to start it, I'd sit in the front and start her up while

Lori and DiDi pushed from the back. When the engine caught, they'd scream and run, run, run to catch up with me. I was never supposed to brake or we'd have to start all over again. Then I'd slide over to shotgun (which is what you call the seat next to the driver) and DiDi or Lori would jump into the driver's seat. After we won that million dollars, I begged DiDi to get us a bright-yellow convertible—just like The Bug. Only a brand-new one, so she wouldn't have to push it every time we wanted to go somewhere.

"The Blue Bomb got us here and we're going to keep her," DiDi announced. "Besides, have you seen the price of gas? We don't need a new car. The Blue Bomb is just for emergencies."

I didn't really think a soccer game and tailgate party was an emergency.

"Good stuff coming through!" DiDi winked at the girls. "And I'm not talking about the fancy tea sandwiches! C'mon and pile in, little chickadees—kick the door. Don't worry, Haven, honey—just haul back and really kick it! Allie and Haven, meet the Blue Bomb!"

"It's so cool!" said Allie.

"I wish we had a car like this," Haven said. "Ours is so . . . boring."

"Really?" I said. It was just the Blue Bomb. Though I guess it *was* pretty cute with those headlight eyes and silver smile.

"Why are you so surprised?" said DiDi. "The Bomb is a real classic, and these girls have taste. Now, if you all will hold on to the basket with the goodies, we're off! Allie Girl, you are in charge of the music!"

Allie started trying to figure out the buttons of the radio, pushing them in and hearing all these funny stations.

Then a twangy voice came on, sounding like it was backed up by a whole church choir.

"Stop!" I said. "DiDi, that's your song—that's Mama's song." I couldn't see DiDi's face, because I was in the back, but her eyes met mine in the rearview mirror.

It's funny how sometimes eyes don't match voices.

"It sure is, but the girls don't want to hear it—Allie, sweetie, find something you like."

"No," I said. "I want to hear Mama's song. Allie, turn it up."

Haven looked a little uncomfortable, but Allie reached for the volume. "Was your mom famous? Is this her singing?"

"No, honey," said DiDi, "it's just the song that Mama and I were named after. It's called 'Delta Dawn.'"

The Blue Bomb hummed along as we sat and listened.

We listened as that girl sang sweet and sorrowful.

Clear and true.

Yodeling out the curly tips of the notes till you were just about ready to cry.

Afterward, we were all quiet.

Haven sat back as the song ended. "She sounded pretty, but also sort of lonely."

"Is that what *D.D.* stands for, DiDi?" asked Allie. "Delta Dawn?"

"Mmm-hmmm."

"Why'd you change? Don't you like your name?"

"Well, a name like Delta Dawn is a lot to live up to, honey. Top country song and all. Sometimes it's just easier to go by a good old regular name."

Allie cocked her head a little to the side. "I liked the song and I like the name Delta Dawn, but I think I like DiDi better."

In the rearview mirror, I noticed that DiDi's eyes matched her voice again when she said, "You know what? I like DiDi better, too."

twenty-five

When we got to the soccer fields, it looked like there was a whole big hoopla going on. Tables and cars, tents and little mini-grills set up everywhere. Coolers with iced sodas and probably champagne and caviar, too. Everybody looked pretty excited for the game, and I guessed they must be, to get there two hours before it even started.

"Looky, there's Trip!" DiDi waved and headed for this big tent with lots of people. "Yoo-hoo! Hey there, Double B!"

I watched as DiDi hurried over to where Trip and Mace were. She gave them a huge three-way bear hug without even putting down her giant basket.

"What's with DiDi and all the double stuff?" Allie asked. "What's Double B?"

"Trip's initials," I said. "His real name's Bradford Breck-inridge." I slowed down. Haven looked back and came to my side.

"Are you okay?" she whispered. "Do you want me to tell them you don't feel well or had to go home or something?"

I gave a little smile. "No, I'm all right."

And then I heard Billy's unmistakable voice shouting, "G-Girl!"

I rushed over and, after a quick high five, I introduced Allie and Haven, who seemed shy but really pleased to be there.

"Hey, Star Girls," said Billy.

I looked over to where DiDi had gone and saw her laughing with Mace. Trip looked up and waved.

I began studying the grass like I had to memorize how many blades there were, but I could tell he was walking toward us.

I turned to Billy and laughed as loud as I could.

"Uh, G—what's so funny?"

"You are," I answered, sensing Trip behind me. "You are probably the funniest person in the entire northeastern part of the United States."

Billy raised his arms above his head in victory. "Yes! The Best of the Northeast!"

"Right. Northeast corner of the parking lot, maybe." Trip was there, looking like his sweet and beautiful self in his soc-cer uniform—like this was just another day. "Hey, G."

I didn't know what to do or say. It's not like I could do what I actually wanted—which was to ask Trip if he liked Mace better than me now. And why he hadn't given me a KOB that week. Instead, I just shrugged.

"Come over for a sec, okay?" he said. "Billy will entertain everyone."

Billy went right into a series of muscleman poses that had the girls in giggles. I began following Trip to his parents' tent. Haven looked over her shoulder at the same time I did and nodded like everything was going to be okay. Maybe it would be.

As we got closer, I noticed this blond woman standing next to Trip's mom. And glaring at DiDi. I slowed down. Who was she?

"DiDi, is it?" The woman's voice was low, but somehow it cut through the chatter.

"Why, yes it is," DiDi said. "You must be Mrs. Tanglewood, Mace's mom, and Mrs. Davis, too, right?" DiDi held out her hand. "So nice to meet you both."

The blond woman was Mace's mom. So I guess Mace was adopted.

I knew what it meant when a little girl was adopted from China. People have to fly around the world to get those babies. No wonder she was so stuck-up. Being whisked away by rich people to go live in a big house with her very own bomb shelter. She'd been made a fuss over since the day her parents got her.

DiDi didn't seem the least bit surprised. Mace had probably told her all about it during one of their marathon girl-talk sessions.

I looked at Mace's mom. Well, adopted or not, it looked like shooting daggers with the eyes runs in the family.

"I have to tell you what great kids you both have," said DiDi. "Trip is such a gentleman. And Mace—well, we have just been hitting it off since she came in for her little makeover— and I really appreciate your letting her stay on after school at the salon this week, helping me sweep and such."

I froze. Trip walked a few more steps before he turned and looked back at me.

"Sweeping hair at the salon?" Mrs. Tanglewood's voice rose for a second. Then she glanced around and quickly lowered it, smoothing her hair back as she turned to Mace. "You said you've been taking the late bus because of Young Entrepreneurs Club."

Mrs. Davis had a hand on her shoulder. "Tish, let's stay calm."

"It's not a big deal." Mace lifted her chin. "I'm just hanging out and helping DiDi and talking to her about things."

Mace was with DiDi every day this week? Sweeping up and yakking away? And that was not a big deal? DiDi would never let me set a toe in her work space. I used to beg her to let me stay and hang out and talk, but she always made me go home early to shut myself up in a room alone with my books.

DiDi was looking back and forth between Mace and her mom. "Macy?" She bent down so she could look her in the face. "You didn't let your parents know you were hanging out at the salon with me?"

"Of course she didn't!" Mrs. Tanglewood said between her teeth. "Do you think I'd let Mace sweep up the hair of our friends? And who are you to dye a child's hair without permission?"

"Mom, stop it," Mace said. "It's a clip-in. I can take it out anytime I want to—I just don't want to. I tried to tell you, but you were too busy shouting at me!"

"Lower your voice, young lady—"

"No, I won't, and maybe for once you'll hear me. You never listen! DiDi listens to me. DiDi asked me what I wanted to look like—the real me—instead of...of just telling me like you do!" Mace was crying. "She's the first person around here—the first grown-up to listen for five seconds to what it feels like to be me!"

DiDi pulled a rumpled tissue out of her pocket. "Here, baby girl, take this—"

Mrs. Tanglewood shoved it back at her. "Mace, we're going home—"

"No!"

"Yes. Where's your father?"

Mrs. Davis looked upset. "Maybe if you and Mace just took a moment to talk—"

"I'm not going anywhere with her!" Mace said, and she pulled away and ran off the field.

"Mace!" called Mrs. Tanglewood. "Come back!" She turned to DiDi. "Look what you've done. Couldn't you find anyone else to lavish your precious time on?"

I gasped and tried to pull my arm away from Trip. I hadn't even realized he had grabbed me and was trying to hold me still. "Let go! Let go of me!"

"G," he said. "Wait—"

"No—"

DiDi looked our way and saw me. "G?" She came rushing over.

"No." I finally wrenched myself away from Trip and faced DiDi. DiDi with her pulled-back curls and tilty nose and curvy lip. DiDi, who had all the time in the world for Mace. And none for me.

I looked her in the eyes like she taught me, so I could Say It Like It Is. "I wish Mama had never died and left me alone with you."

There's a word I learned in science class:

Implode.

It means to sort of blow up and collapse. But, like, quietly, from the inside. I knew what it meant in science class. I had just never seen it before in real life—till I saw it in DiDi's face.

Pull-Aparts

This is what you call Pull-Apart Bread. Everyone wants a piece of it, so when it shows up, you better just get in there and grab what you want.

- ⅔ cup white sugar
- ⅔ cup light brown sugar
- 1 tablespoon cinnamon
- 4 cans of Mayflower refrigerator biscuits
- 8 ounces cream cheese

Preheat your oven to 350°F.

Put your sugars and cinnamon in a big plastic bag and shake it up. One can at a time, toss in your refrigerator biscuits and shake them all around till each one is completely coated with sugar. Lightly butter the inside of a 12-cup Bundt pan. Line the bottom and sides of the pan with 3 cans of the biscuits. The entire inside of the pan should be covered in biscuits, leaving a circular ditch.

Cut your cream cheese into cubes and fill the entire inside of the ditch. Sprinkle some of the leftover sugar mix over the cream cheese. Use the last can of biscuits to cover and seal the top of the ditch.

Bake at 350°F for 40 minutes, or till everything is golden brown and a toothpick comes out clean. Let the Pull-Aparts cool for 5 minutes, then flip them onto a plate. Sprinkle the last of the cinnamon sugar over the soft oozy top.

Oh, and please eat while it's nice and warm! Whenever I serve this, folks go crazy pulling that bread apart looking for the best piece. But the truth is, there's no need to pull so hard. There's enough for everyone.

Serves 10–12.

twenty-six

Yes, we live in a Walking Town.

But it still felt like a long, long way from school back to Main Street.

When I got to the apartment, I trudged up the stairs, wiping my tears and snotty nose on my sleeve, and then I did it again on the other side just to spite DiDi because I knew she hated it. I didn't even bother putting myself on Kenneth Alert. Who cared? He wanted to see DiDi, not me. I reached the top and stopped short. Someone was sitting on the floor. It was Mace.

She looked like she'd been crying, too, but before I could ask what she was doing leaning against our apartment door, she started talking.

"I'm sorry I've been so—so mean. It's just—it's just Trip and I have known each other since we were little. We were always together. Then last summer, this—there was this stupid thing—and since then, it's been weird and he just—and then you show up and, just like that, you're his best friend."

Stupid thing? Me, Trip's best friend?

"And that makes up for the nasty way you've been treating me? Making smart remarks about my mama? Picking on DiDi, and then suddenly you're working with her and hanging out and t-talking all the time—and it's like—" My voice cracked. "It's like you're spending more time with DiDi than I am...."

Mace was looking me straight in the face, and at that moment, I had to give her credit. Most people, probably including me, would be looking down at the ground during a talk like this.

"Okay." She nodded. "I did go there to give DiDi a hard time, but then—she was so nice and—and started talking to me about how I wanted to look and asking who I thought I was on the inside and how maybe we could make my hair match the way I feel."

I said nothing.

"Anyway, I know you didn't mean what you said that day outside the nurse's office.... I know DiDi likes me. We—we talk all the time now at the salon. She lets me do all sorts of things there. Not that I think I could do what she does or ever be as good as she is. It's just..." She shook her head. "All my mom does is try to make me what *she* wants me to be."

As long as I could remember, DiDi had been telling me what she wanted me to be.

Not asking me. Telling me.

I could feel a tiny part of me thinking that, maybe, Mace and I had something in common.

Then I stopped myself. Because we didn't.

Maybe we had both just run away from people who were telling us what to do and who to be. But I didn't have anybody on my side, and it looked like she had DiDi. And now she had Trip back, too.

Then Mace with her rock star haircut looked up at me with my DiDi Special. Her mouth still and waiting, like it wasn't sure whether or not it should stay in a straight, straight line.

I stepped past her into the apartment and clicked the door shut. Then I locked it.

twenty-seven

The whole next week, words between me and DiDi were dry and crumbly like week-old bread. She would step into the room sometimes when I was studying. Stand there a moment, then turn and walk away.

At the lunch table, Mace wouldn't even look at me.

I heard myself yammering away about this and that, but none of it mattered. Trip watched and watched me and didn't say anything, then at the end of one day passed me a KOB that said, *Open Now—Are you okay?* I nodded and smiled my fake-cheese smile. Haven came to my locker to see if a Stargazers meeting would make me feel better, but I told her I had too much homework. Poor Billy, every time he came looking for high fives, all I had to give him were low ones.

Halloween used to be my favorite time of year, but I couldn't even imagine going out with everyone and acting like everything was all fine. Luckily, it landed in the middle of the week, and I used the excuse that I had too much homework and DiDi wouldn't let me go.

By Friday, I wasn't even looking forward to the weekend. Between staying home with DiDi and being in the same school as Mace, I didn't know which was worse. Especially since the last two times Mace and I talked, I had pretty much shut a door in her face.

"Hey, G." Trip had run to catch up with me in the hall before last period.

"Um, hey." I tried to make my voice sound as natural as possible. I really just wanted to get out of there.

He pushed the hair off his face. "Do you want to come over?" Then he nudged me and smiled. "I promise, no zombie movies. We'll just...we can do whatever you want...."

My eyes started to sting. "Really?"

He nodded. He wasn't saying it, but I knew he wanted to be there for me. That it was hard for him to see me have that fight with DiDi. That it was important for him to help make me feel better. He didn't say it. And he didn't write it. But I still knew.

Then I thought about his mom and Mace's mom. The best friends who were probably teamed up against me and DiDi. "But will your mom mind? You know, with all the stuff..."

"My parents are doing some spa getaway, and they asked Rosa to stay at the house. So it's just you and me. We'll get pizza and talk and just hang out. Okay?"

I nodded.

"Good. I guess we have to ask DiDi?"

We had barely spoken all week, but now I would have to talk to her. And she would have to answer.

"We'll stop there after school. She'll say yes." He pointed to himself and gave me a crooked smile. "Remember? The power of Perfect Boy."

"Yeah, yeah. DiDi is a fan. Don't get a big head."

"Meet you out front after last period."

"Okay. And, Trip?"

"Yes?"

"Just . . . thank you."

Walking through town with Trip, I could feel my chest begin to fill up with the kind of light and air that only comes when you have something good to look forward to. If I could get by the next few minutes with DiDi, then nothing could go wrong. You'd think a brain like me would've figured out by now it doesn't work that way.

Mace was in the salon with DiDi. She and the other stylists were gathered around and talking. That happy feeling flew out of me like someone had left the back door open.

"Trip!" DiDi called out. "How's the handsomest boy in town?"

"Hi, DiDi."

"Oh, you charmer, get over here. We're going to order a pizza. Do you want to join us? Hey, Double—I mean Leia." DiDi's voice got quieter.

"Hey, DiDi," I said softly. For some reason, I thought about her staying in that tent all night in a storm so I could go to the best school possible.

Trip turned to me. "Do you want to? You know, just hang here?" He watched my face in that studying way he had.

"Oh. Well. If you want. It's just . . . we were going to watch a movie at Trip's house . . . if it's okay with you, D."

DiDi waved a hand. "Oh, that sounds more fun. Mace, honey, go on and join—" She stopped herself. Like she'd just remembered that very second that the girl she was hanging out with was mortal enemies with her own flesh and blood.

I could feel my hands clenching into fists. Any piece of me feeling warm again toward DiDi was gone.

Mace didn't even glance my way. "I think I'll stay here. I'm just not in the movie mood."

DiDi looked from me to Mace, and I didn't know why she looked so sad. "Okay, then. Have fun. Do you need me to drive you in the Blue Bomb?"

"That's okay," Trip said. "We have time to catch the late

bus there and our housekeeper, Rosa, can bring G home. Thanks, DiDi."

DiDi reached up and pushed the hair out of his face like she'd done the first time she met him. "Well, thank *you*."

Back at Trip's house, it was like I could breathe again. We hung out and talked and ordered a pizza, which Rosa put out on the dining table for us with plain old paper plates and paper napkins.

"Let's go to the hill," Trip said after dinner. "I don't want to miss the sunset."

Sunsets on Trip's hill were something else. The sky over the water turned pink and purple like they were the only two colors in the world. We lay in the grass, looking up at the wide world, thinking that nothing could ever be better.

"G-Girl," Trip said into the sky.

"Mmm-hmm."

"Are you...do you want to talk about...you know..."

I shook my head.

"You can if you want...."

"I know," I said. "And I know you'll listen and—thank you for that." I'd never realized what it was like to have someone always listen to me, till this year with Trip. And maybe that was a good thing and maybe that was a bad thing, because it also made me realize how much I wished DiDi did.

"Sometimes I feel like all you do is listen to me yak away. I wouldn't blame you if you were—well, if you wanted to hang out with someone who didn't talk so much...."

Trip didn't say anything.

"And DiDi—" I paused. "Well, she says no one likes going down a one-way street all the time...so, you know...I'm a good listener, too."

We lay there a little longer in the quiet purple, not saying a word.

I heard him sit up, so I did the same. We sat there, cross-legged, facing each other.

He reached out one finger and touched my forehead. "I like your star."

I reached up and rubbed it. "Oh. Well, you know, I used to hate it, but DiDi says being born with a birthmark like this is like a sign. That I was meant to study the stars like Mama did—well, like the way she wanted to, I mean."

"I like that it's white...and a star. I always think of birthmarks as just brown blotches. I have one on my knee, but it's not shaped like anything cool. Well, Billy thinks it looks like Florida."

We were quiet again. We were so close, our knees were right up next to each other. Barely touching. Then he reached into his pocket and pulled out a bent-up KOB. It looked like maybe it had been in there for a while.

There was nothing written on the outside. "Wait till I get home?" I said.

He paused for a long time. "Just...wait. Can you not open it till I ask?"

I nodded and took a deep breath. His Wish Pie eyes were so close. As we sat there just sort of looking at each other, time passed by. Pure and perfect. I thought about how I'd never even come close to kissing a boy before. I closed my eyes and leaned forward.

"Trip? Leia? Is that you?" Trip's mom and dad were marching up the hill toward us. They each had a cocktail in their Giant Supply Store glasses. I guess you don't have to go back for as many refills when your glass is that big.

I scrambled up, thinking about how it looked, Trip and I with our faces almost touching.

"Trip, Dad and I are having the—we're having friends over for a late dinner. We can take Leia home before they get here."

"But we wanted to watch a movie—and aren't you supposed to be at a spa weekend or something?"

Trip's dad gave me this weak look. If DiDi had been there, she probably would have said something about pants and who was wearing them and who wasn't. I straightened up right away. "Aw, it's no problem. DiDi likes when I'm home early anyway."

But all I wanted was to be on that hillside with Trip.

"Thank you, Leia," said Mrs. Davis.

I grabbed each side of my mouth with imaginary fingers and pulled as hard as I could till I was smiling back.

twenty-eight

The next day, I zipped by DiDi in the kitchen and mumbled something about going to the library, but instead, I walked through town by myself. I thought about being on the hill with Trip. I thought about how alone I felt. And then I thought about it some more. And then in the middle of all that thinking, I saw the reflection of a woman in a store window. She paused ahead of me on the sidewalk. She seemed to glance back at me and then stop and look again. She turned and asked a passerby something. She looked lost.

I knew the lost woman was not Mama.

I knew because she was alive and my mama was dead.

But I followed her anyway. Just for a bit. Because truth is, right at that moment, I really needed a little What If.

I watched from down the street as she ducked into this little store. I waited a minute and then followed her in.

The door made a pretty little bell sound. I stepped inside and closed my eyes. It smelled like candles and perfume and fancy paper.

"May I help you?"

I heard myself answer, "Do you carry Revlon's Cherries in the Snow lipstick? In the Classic Gold Case, please?"

I opened my eyes.

The salesclerk was an older woman. Not like Granny Old. More like Older Aunt Old. She had on this pretty sweater with a little gold chain that held it together in the front. I looked around for the woman who was Not Mama. She had gone straight to the counter in the back and was talking to a man about some kind of skin cream.

The salesclerk in the pretty sweater peered at me over her little glasses, but her voice was kind. "I believe that shade has been out of production for quite a while now. Years, actually. How do you even know it?"

Our eyes met. And the way she smiled at me, right then and there, I just knew she didn't have a stopwatch in her pocket.

I started talking. "It was my mama's favorite lipstick. The only one she'd ever wear. If she went into a drugstore and they were out of it, she'd go into the next one and the next one and the—next." My voice started to squeak. I did that trick where you keep your eyes open real wide. Trying not to blink, because I really did not want to cry in front of this nice lady with the pretty sweater, held by a gold chain. "At least, that's what my sister, DiDi, always said."

The woman nodded. "I'm Ida." She held out her hand. Then she held out a tissue.

"Hi, Miss Ida, it's nice to meet you." I took a deep breath. "My name is Galileo."

"Galileo? Ah! After Galileo the scientist?"

I nodded.

"A heavenly name. Far more appropriate for a pretty young girl than an old man, if you ask me."

"Well, truth is I never liked it, but DiDi always calls me GiGi…till this year. I, um, kind of decided to try being called—Leia." I wasn't sure why I was talking to her like this or why it mattered what she thought. "Do you—like it?"

"I do," Ida said right away. Like she'd made up her mind in that second. "You're taking charge of your own destiny, and I like that very much. Highly commendable in a young person."

I exhaled and looked around. The Cottage Pharmacy. With a whole counter of beautifully shaped soaps and hair clips and even some shiny jewelry. Ida didn't look like a real drugstore clerk. I mean, she looked like a real person, but maybe like a real person on a TV show about real people who are better looking and better dressed than most real people.

Which, to tell the truth, was pretty much the way this whole town looked.

"You know…" Ida tapped her chin with a finger. "I do remember a customer who came in here talking about a lipstick that she wanted—one that had been discontinued… hmmm."

The lady who was Not Mama had paid the cashier and was now heading for the door.

I turned my head.

She walked out.

I began to take a step in her direction. Then stopped.

Ida was looking at me like she was trying to figure something out. "Teddy?" she called. "Will you cover the front of the store for a bit? I'm just going to be in my office with Leia here."

This nice young man peeked around the aisle. He waved at me and said, "No problem, Ida."

And the next thing you know, we were behind the counter and going through this door with a big bulletin board that had crisscrossing pink and green ribbons all over it, held down with bright brass tacks. Stuck between the ribbons were all these photos and notes. Now, I'm not sure why anyone would ever send mail to their drugstore, but the Cottage Pharmacy had tons.

Birth announcements!

Thank-you cards!

It just made me happy that Ida was letting me come into her office. I'll bet none of those people thanking her were invited back there. On the doorknob, there was a sign hanging from a ribbon with a tiny patchwork frame that had the words PRIVATE! PLEASE KEEP OUT! in tiny little pink stitches. Why, even her KEEP OUT sign was pretty and polite.

The door led to a little hallway where there was a coffee machine and a little basket of mini-muffins. A restroom. ("Do you need to use the ladies', Leia?" to which I answered, "No thank you, ma'am.") And a glass door at the far end, which led to the back parking lot. Right before that was a plain door that said EMPLOYEES ONLY.

Ida took out a key and opened the door. I guess I expected the office to be as pretty and decorated as everything else, but I have to say it was mostly businesslike. A big computer and stacks and stacks of notebooks and little pieces of scribbly paper stuck everywhere. Boxes were piled up in one corner— some opened, with those little foam peanuts spilling out. I loved foam peanuts. Whenever I could get ahold of them, I'd use them to torture DiDi. She was terrified of the sound they made rubbing and squeaking together. It always made her scream and run away, laughing hysterically. But it never bothered me. Funny, the things people run away from.

"Here, Leia," Ida said. "Take a seat and let's see if we can at least get you started."

She turned on her computer, which began to hum nicely and then gave a little piano chord. Like it was ready to play.

She glanced up at me. "Did you ever try a quick Internet search?"

"No." I shook my head. I wasn't sure how to explain. "I just—I knew it wasn't anywhere. I knew. But this part of me"—I pointed to my heart—"this place inside me just... liked wishing, and asking for it. I've never had anything of my mama's, and I know it's just... lipstick, but it feels more like... it feels more like I'd be finding a piece of her. And that would be a miracle."

Ida looked at me with her kind eyes. "Miracles and lipstick. I like it."

"And then right before we moved here, this No-Good Lying Son of a Walnut who was dating our friend Lori, he said that sometimes companies bring back old colors....I didn't think much of it. But then this girl I know—my friend Haven—she said the same thing. So for the very first time, I thought maybe I could really find it. And if I could get it— really and truly get it—then it would be like Mama coming back and bringing me and DiDi together again and everything would—" I hiccupped. "It would fix everything, Miss Ida. I just know it."

Ida nodded and gave me a moment of quiet before she

started talking again. I appreciated it. "Well, what your No-Good Son of a Walrus was talking about—"

"Walnut."

"Really? Well, Walnut, then—though personally, I find Son of a Walrus more humorous. What he was talking about is what we call a reissue."

"Reissue?"

"It means that for a limited time, a company may celebrate a popular retired color by selling it in stores again." She started typing quickly on the keyboard.

"Really?" I asked. And I held my breath.

"Look at this," Ida said.

The screen began filling up top to bottom with hundreds of ideas about where I could find Cherries in the Snow. It was crazy.

"Miss Ida?"

"Hmmm—yes, dear?"

I paused. "DiDi and I had a fight. Well, we've had a couple of fights lately. And I think, well, I know I said some pretty mean things to her."

Ida was watching me. Really close. But I liked the way she was doing it. Not like some pie judge, trying to see what kind of pie I was from the outside. But more like maybe she wanted to know what kind I was on the inside. And like it was important to her.

"I thought if I got her Cherries in the Snow for her birthday, then we'd both—we'd always have part of Mama with us. Do you think she'd like that?"

I don't know why Ida would know. But I just wanted her to like my idea while I was in that messy office inside the beautiful store where there was a pink-and-green-ribboned door covered with thank-you notes and a polite way to say KEEP OUT.

"I can't imagine a lovelier gift," said Ida. "I do have to get back to the store, but you are more than welcome to stay here and search online as long as you'd like."

I looked at that list of all the places Cherries in the Snow lipstick was waiting to be found. "Is it okay—could I please just print this? I-I think I want to do this with some—some friends I have."

Ida smiled and pressed Print. A fresh, smooth, miraculous sheet of paper flew practically right into the air. Ida caught it and handed it to me. "Friends are always a good idea."

The paper was light and cool and perfect. "Thank you, Miss Ida."

She held out her hand. I held out mine and we shook.

"I hope you find what you're looking for," she said.

twenty-nine

The next day was Sunday. I called Haven, figuring I would start off like it was all about the Stargazers, but I knew what I really wanted. What I needed. To call places on that list from Miss Ida without DiDi around. And the truth was I wouldn't mind talking about what had happened with Trip on that hill while the sun was setting. Wasn't that what having girls who were friends was all about? I guess what I needed was someone to talk about Girl Stuff.

As a rule, DiDi and I don't buy each other gifts. If there's any extra money at the end of the month, DiDi sticks it in my college fund, which I think she's had around since I was in preschool. So whenever it's our birthdays, DiDi will say,

"Happy birthday, Double G, I just put one percent of your college tuition in the bank."

Every year on my birthday, she'll make the prettiest Twinkie Pie ever and say it's for both of us, but nine days later, when her birthday comes around, she never wants me to make a fuss. Then she spends the day sitting in front of a mirror staring at herself. It's a fact: Good-looking people sure can be weird about getting old.

But this year, things were going to be different. I was going to make sure DiDi had a gift this year. The best gift ever. It was like Mama had left me a path to follow. My star birthmark. The Stargazers. Miss Ida. And finding Cherries in the Snow. I was going to get DiDi that lipstick. Like I'd told Miss Ida, I just knew in my heart that if we had a little bit of Mama with us, things would be better.

I cleared my throat three times while Haven's phone was ringing.

Haven picked up. "Hey!"

I sighed in relief.

"Hi. Haven. Um. It's G—uh—it's Leia."

"I know, Leia. You're kind of the only person who doesn't just text me. What's up?"

Even though I was just about bursting with wanting to

talk about the list and Trip, I figured the Recipe for Success would have me play it cool, so I didn't sound so needy and desperate. Then maybe after we'd finished all our Stargazers stuff, I'd find a way to work in everything else.

"I was just thinking we should meet—today—and discuss some of our plans for the Stargazers and what some of, um, our next goals are."

There was this long pause.

"Oh...um...I guess we could do that, but..."

My heart tumbled down the stairs to my toes. "Don't worry about it," I said. "We don't have to—it was just an idea."

"I'm sorry—I'm just not in the mood to do school stuff today."

"It's okay....Listen, I'll just see you—"

"Do you—would you like to come over and just hang out instead?"

My heart peeked out from its sad heap on the floor. "Really?"

"Only—only if you want."

"I do! I—I mean, sure. That'd be cool."

"Okay, great. I'll text Al. Then maybe we can go to a movie or shopping—or just do girl stuff."

"Girl Stuff." I wondered if Haven could hear the smile on my face. "Girl Stuff would be—perfect. I'll ask DiDi to drop me off in a little bit—if that's okay."

"Anytime is okay."

"Thanks! See you then."

"See you, Leia."

Sometimes things that you think are going to be hard turn out to be easier than pie.

Easier-Than-Pie Pudding

- 2 boxes of instant vanilla pudding mix
- 4 cups milk (for pudding)
- 1 box of chocolate wafers
- Your favorite creamy peanut butter
- 3 bananas, sliced
- An 8-ounce tub of whipped topping

Everyone thinks this dessert is a whole big production, but really it's easier than pie.

Go on and make the pudding. Do I have to explain how? Beat the pudding mix and milk with a whisk for 2 minutes. Then just let it rest there for a spell. 'Cause if you ask me, it's hard work being pudding.

Get yourself a nice 9-by-9-inch glass dish and start layering your ingredients. Spread each of your chocolate wafers with a thin smear of peanut butter. Lay them on the bottom of the dish, peanut butter side up. Then add a layer of pudding. Sliced bananas. Whipped topping. Repeat till you reach the top. End with a layer of whipped topping. Crush a handful of chocolate wafers and sprinkle over the top.

Put it in the fridge for several hours, till firm.

Now, what could be easier than that?

Serves 8–10.

thirty

When DiDi found out that Haven was having me and Allie over, she wanted me to take the Easier-Than-Pie Pudding she had in the fridge.

"I was going to bring it to the salon for everyone to munch, but I'd much rather you and your new girlfriends enjoy it."

I could tell DiDi was working hard to make things okay between us. Like they hadn't been since Mace's haircut. Or the tailgate. Or, pretty much, since we moved here.

"Okay."

"Okay, then."

"…Thank you."

"Anytime, G—I mean, anytime, Leia."

At Haven's house, the girls just about did flips over the pudding. Instead of serving it all formal, like in Giant crystal goblets, Haven just handed each of us a soup spoon and shouted, "On your marks! Get set! Go!" And we all dug into the middle of it, scooping and gobbling as fast as we could. It was fun and silly and just about everything I always wanted to have with girlfriends.

I only got to meet Haven's dad, since her mom was traveling again. He had just brought Haven's little brother back from his kindergarten swim class. I thought he was the cutest little thing ever, but Haven assured me there was a reason she called him the Beast. I thought her dad might be the shy and nervous type like she was, but he was actually really friendly and goofy and kept trying to hang out and joke around till Haven got all embarrassed and begged him to leave us alone.

All I have to say is that Girl Stuff is *F, U, N*, FUN.

We listened to all of Haven's music and danced around the room.

We went through last year's yearbook and talked about which boys were cute and which weren't.

Her dad kept bringing us snacks and drinks and then more snacks, which the Beast kept trying to steal, but Haven said he was on a strict diet to keep him from being hyper and wasn't allowed to snack between meals.

At one point, Allie said something about the tailgate, and Haven nudged her and quickly changed the subject. Allie slapped a hand over her own mouth, and it got a little awkward. This is the weird thing. It also made me feel glad. I took it to mean that they had decided ahead of time not to mention anything about it—even though they had seen the whole fight with DiDi and Mace's mom. That they wanted today to be just about making me happy, and I don't think anyone had ever done that for me before.

We decided to start trying on all the clothes in Haven's closet, which honestly, I didn't really get. I mean, why would you try on someone else's clothes? But Haven and Allie seemed to want to do it, so I went along. Allie wanted to start with fancy party dresses, so Haven handed me one that was sort of silvery white and swirly, with little straps on the shoulders. I had never had anything like it. Of course, since I'm the size of a peanut, it was way too long and really roomy on me you-know-where, but it was beautiful. Then Haven got out this huge crate of makeup, and we put on pink blush and glossy lips and sparkly eye shadow.

"You look soooo pretty!" Haven said, standing beside me in the mirror. She was wearing this fluffy pink number that looked like one of Mama's desserts. Allie was in yellow.

"Yeah?" I looked at my reflection, and I have to admit it was nice not looking like a little kid for once. "I guess I kind of feel pretty."

"No wonder Trip lo-o-o-o-ves you," Allie said.

I could feel my face go all hot and red. "He's doesn't. Really—we're just—he's—"

Haven looked at me in the mirror. "It's okay if a boy likes you, Leia. Just because Trip is chasing after you doesn't mean anyone thinks you're chasing him back."

"Do you...do you really think he's—chasing me?" I looked again at my reflection.

Allie popped a mini–chocolate chip cookie into her mouth and brushed the crumbs off her fingertips. "Well, that's pretty much what everyone is saying, so..."

Haven grinned. "Did you ever kiss?"

"No!" I yelled. Then I hid my face in my hands and moaned while the two of them crowded around me.

Allie kept poking me and saying, "She did! She did! Admit it!"

I lowered my voice even though no one else was even close to hearing. I knew this was true, because Haven's house was bigger than a bowling alley and she had a whole wing to herself. "Well, I thought—maybe—he was going to Friday at his house, but then his parents came home."

"That is so embarrassing!" said Allie. "What did you do?"

"Nothing. It was time for me to go home anyway."

"You know, he kissed Mace last summer."

I went still.

The kind of still where you're trying so hard not to move

that all you can think about is that you don't know what the heck to do with your hands. They felt like birds that wanted to flap around and take off. I stuck them behind my back.

"They—I didn't know."

Mace had said they were just friends. Was she lying?

Haven gave Allie a look. "It wasn't a real one. It was during this stupid game at a party. Someone wanted to play Spin the Bottle and they kissed. They had to. It's, like, in the rules. I don't even think he wanted to."

"Yeah...probably not a big deal," I managed to say.

I could feel Haven and Allie looking at each other.

I shrugged and tried to act all light. "Anyway, DiDi says there's plenty of time for kissing when I'm married."

"I'm not waiting that long!" Haven threw herself on the bed dramatically.

"Me either," said Allie, falling next to Haven.

"Me either," I said, flopping between them. I gave this little fake laugh and tried not to think about Trip and Mace kissing. I just wanted to change the subject. And suddenly, I knew exactly what I wanted to change it to.

I sat up. "Will you help me with something?"

"Yes! Yes!" Haven and Allie scrambled up and started jumping on the bed. "Is it Boy Stuff?" said Allie.

"No." I smacked her on the arm. "It's—remember I told you about the...about my mama's lipstick?"

"Yes," Allie sighed. "Strawberries and Snow!"

194

Haven laughed. "Nice try, Al—it was Cherries, right? I texted my mom about it. She said she'd ask some people after she got back next week."

Allie shrugged. "Cherries, strawberries. Who cares? It still sounds like dessert."

"Well, I want to get it for DiDi—"

"Yes! For her birthday!" Allie said.

"We don't usually give gifts, because DiDi is all nuts about saving for my college tuition and all—" I stopped talking. It suddenly felt like Haven's entire beautiful house had ears and was listening to every word I was saying. The girls had been to our apartment and had seen that DiDi slept on the sofa. It was pretty obvious you couldn't find a swirly silver dress in my closet if you hired a detective.

I took a breath and ran back to where I'd dropped my jeans on the floor and pulled Ida's printout from the pocket. It was all folded and rumply. "Well, I got this list of places that sell old lipstick—"

Allie wrinkled her nose.

"Okay, okay. Remember I told you it doesn't mean old like Old. They're what you call a Special Reissue. I figure I can buy DiDi a whole box of them and it won't matter that—" My eyes stung with tears. "Nothing will matter, because it'll be like we have a piece of Mama with us every day."

The girls paused a moment, and I could tell that they weren't pausing because it was awkward, but because they wanted to give me a moment of silence, like teachers do in school when they want to show that something is too big for words. My heart swelled wide as the sky.

"She'll love it," said Haven.

Allie looked serious. "This isn't just a birthday gift, Leia. This is a mission in memory of your mom. It's, like, big-time important."

Haven was all ready to start searching on her laptop, when Allie said, "Wait, I have a better idea! Let me see the first number." And she pulled out her cell phone with a wicked grin. When the poor person on the other end answered, she had the entire conversation in a dead-on imitation of Mace's mom, ending with a big "What do you mean, you don't carry that color? That's preposterous! My daughter is president of the Young Entrepreneurs Club, and she could teach you a thing or two!" We all ended up collapsed on the bed, screaming and laughing hysterically.

Haven went next, holding her nose and trying to talk in this whiny, high-pitched voice, but she couldn't stop herself from cracking up every other word. It was so funny I didn't even care that the answer to that call was no, they didn't have Cherries in the Snow, either. Next to the times I'd spent with Trip, this was probably the happiest I'd been since moving here.

"Okay, my turn!" I reached for the phone. I knew there was one thing I was good at and that was pretending to be DiDi.

The girls were tickling me and trying to make me laugh. I wiggled away. "Stop it, now. I'm getting into character." I dialed the next number on the list. Classic Cosmetics, Inc.

It rang three times and then this woman answered. I could tell by her voice that she was more than thrilled to be spending her time telling me about old makeup. "Good-afternoon-and-thank-you-for-calling-Classic-Cosmetics-this-is-Jamie-your-sales-associate-how-can-I-help-you-today?"

I cleared my throat. "Why, good afternoon. I'm looking to order some of Revlon's Cherries in the Snow lipstick. Please."

Allie whispered, "Demand to speak to the supervising buyer!"

"Shut up!" Haven said. They started throwing cookies at each other.

I could hear Jamie clicking away on her keyboard.

Click, click, clickety, click, click, click.

"Yes, ma'am. It looks like the original Revlon's Cherries in the Snow Super Lustrous formula was discontinued some time ago—"

"Oh well, thank you—"

"However, Revlon does occasionally reissue the Classic Gold Case—and—"

Clickety, clickety, click, click.

"And we currently have them in stock. How many did you want?"

"Wait." My voice caught. The cookies stopped flying

through the air. "You—you have it? You really have it?" The girls screamed and started jumping up and down on the bed.

"Are you over eighteen years of age, ma'am?"

I waved my arms for them to quiet down. "Yes. Yes, absolutely."

"Name of the person we will be shipping to, please."

"Ahem." I grinned at the girls. "This is Delta Dawn Barnes."

Click, click, click, clickety, click.

"Spell the last name, please."

"*B, A, R, N, E, S.*"

I raised my fist in the air and the girls went into this silent version of a screaming cheer.

"And how will you be paying today, Ms. Barnes?"

"Wha—uh . . . pay?" I looked at the girls.

Allie jumped up and whispered, "I have my bag downstairs with my emergency credit card! And, girlfriend—" She stuck out a hip and snapped her fingers. "This is an emergency!"

I reached out and squeezed her tight. "Get out!"

"*Mmf!*—Get where?"

I laughed. "Out. It's just this thing DiDi and I—oh, never mind—thank you, thank you, thank you! I'll pay you back with babysitting money!" We hugged again and Allie ran downstairs. "I'll have that credit card in just two minutes, ma'am!" I sang into the phone.

Sales Associate Jamie was just out of her mind with excitement over my improved financial situation. "That's fine, Miss Barnes. While we're waiting, you can give me the name and address of the credit card holder."

"Sure thing," I said, and gave her Allie's information while Haven and I did a little hula dance in celebration.

Click, click, clickety-click, clickety-clickety-click.

Sales Associate Jamie repeated everything to me. "Is that correct?"

"Yes! Yes! All correct!"

It's funny how sometimes things just come together so perfectly. Eating Easier-Than-Pie Pudding. Doing Girl Stuff with Haven and Allie. And finally, finally, really and truly, finding Mama's lipstick. I felt just about ready to burst. It reminded me of when Mr. McGuire told us about this theory on how the universe was born. It was something about there being so much good stuff like stars and planets and galaxies all bunched up together in one teeny-tiny place that it was just a matter of time before it all exploded and we found ourselves in the real world like it is now. The Big Bang, it was called. The explosion that changed everything.

Click, click, clickety-click, clickety-clickety-click.

"And will we be shipping there as well, Miss Barnes, or would you prefer the Red Cedar Road address?"

At that second, Allie came back into the room doing this

really funny super-slow-motion run and holding up that credit card like it was the Olympic torch. Haven waved her in, making a noise like roaring crowds.

I almost swallowed my head whole, trying not to spit into the phone. "I—I'm sorry, ma'am—Cedar who?"

Click.

Click.

Clack.

"We have on record here that a month ago, we delivered a dozen Revlon's Cherries in the Snow lipsticks to a Miss Delta Dawn Barnes at 39 Red Cedar Road, Verity, South Carolina. This is you, Miss Barnes, isn't it?"

"...Miss Barnes?"

thirty-one

Sometimes when you look at a phone, it just doesn't make sense. I mean, it's this little piece of plastic that you hold while people tell you impossible things.

"Are you there, ma'am?"

Haven and Allie were watching me.

"What?" I said. "What..." It was like I had Gone Grammatical in a bad dream where the words couldn't come out. "Just...never mind."

"You wish to cancel the order, Miss Barnes?"

"I don't...yes."

"That's no problem. Thank you for shopping at Classic. Will you stay on the line to answer a few questions for our customer survey—"

I hung up.

Haven and Allie were standing at my shoulders. Haven reached out a hand.

"What happened?"

I couldn't speak. I went into the bathroom, looked in the mirror, and said to myself over and over, *39 Red Cedar Road, 39 Red Cedar Road, 39 Red Cedar Road. Verity, South Carolina*. I put down the top of the toilet seat so I could sit and think.

Verity was where our old trailer burned down.

Verity was the last place where Mama had been alive.

Verity was where we lived before we moved in with Lori. Verity was—I tried to make sense of everything that was churning and tumbling in my head, but all I could think was...

What If.

Impossible Pie

- 2 cups milk
- ½ cup Mayflower baking mix (or Bisquick works fine, too)
- ½ stick butter, softened
- 4 eggs
- 1 teaspoon vanilla
- 1¼ cups sugar
- A 7-ounce bag of sweetened flaked coconut

This is the thing. Sometimes you think something is impossible, but it turns out it's completely possible. You just need to look. Seriously, in your pantry this whole time you've had the ingredients to make pie. Just look at this list. I will bet it's all in there right now!

Put the first 6 ingredients into a blender in the order listed. Blend for 3 minutes. Add the coconut, and give it another quick blend till mixed. Pour into a greased 9-inch pie pan and bake for 45 minutes at 350°F.

Put a knife in the center. If it comes out clean, it's done. See? You had it the whole time. You just never knew.

Serves 8.

thirty-two

When I came out, I told Haven and Allie I didn't feel well and asked if someone could drive me home. Haven's dad brought me back into town. It was late afternoon and I knew that the salon closed early on Sundays, and I needed to ask DiDi about 39 Red Cedar Road.

I needed her to explain the mistake.

I needed her to have an answer.

I needed her to tell me one of her long-winded yakkity stories, and this one time, I'd be glad to hear it and then annoyed that she was talking so much and then everything would be back to normal.

At the salon, I could see through the glass doors that Clarisse had gone home. DiDi usually stayed in the back, cleaning up and talking with the other stylists before leaving. As I walked in, I could hear soft voices.

"I know it's hard, sweetheart, but being yourself—all it means is letting everyone out there see what's true in here."

I peeked around the corner and saw DiDi gently touching the top of Mace's head. The floor creaked and DiDi saw me.

"Well, hey there, Double—I mean Leia. I didn't expect you back yet from Haven's house."

I turned around and walked out.

I went straight up the stairs to our apartment. As I shoved the key into the lock, I could hear Kenneth's door open. Without turning around, I slammed our door shut. Why was it my job to be nice to him? He was the one mooning after DiDi even though she didn't give him a speck of time. How long would it take him to get it through his dumb old ponytailed head that DiDi didn't care about him? At all.

I washed my face and brushed my teeth and put on an old prescription pain relief T-shirt that Lori had given me from when she was dating this pharmaceutical salesman. Boy, we thought she'd hit the jackpot then. She kept saying, "See you later, ladies. I'm probably off to Vegas for a bunch of fancy conventions and buffet dinners."

But it didn't work out. He left town just as quickly as he'd come, and whenever anyone asked about him, Lori would say, "Nothing but a pipe dream, girls. Some things are just too good to be true. You try to grab hold and they slip away."

DiDi came in.

"GiGi! What happened? Mace and I were really worried about you."

I'll bet.

I climbed into bed. If she wanted to spend her time with Mace, let her.

"Isn't it kind of early for bed? Did you even have dinner?"

I didn't answer.

"Okay...Well, I have to drive Macy home. It's been a little rough with her mom—"

I pulled the covers over my head.

"Anyway, I'll be back later if you want to talk."

Talk? When did we ever talk? When did we ever talk about anything except for how to turn the recipe of my life into a triple-layer Success Cake?

I heard her back out of the room. "So...just leave your light on if you want me to come in later. I'll be back in—"

I jumped up and had the light off before she could finish her sentence.

They used to tell this story about Dead Drunk Donna. That when she was upset, she would leave the lights in her trailer on all night and howl at the moon. Singing and howling and clutching that shotgun full of golden bullets. With no one to listen to her except maybe that dead bear tied to a tree.

Monday morning in English class, I walked straight to Trip and said in a low voice, "Can you meet me in the library after my volunteer job?"

He looked at me, all serious. Studying me in that way he had. I guess something in my face let him know that this wasn't going to be about homework.

"Are you—"

I shook my head. I didn't want to say anything else. The idea of Mama and the lipstick and everything was tied up so tight in my brain, I was afraid that one pull would bring the whole thing down into a tangled mess, right in the middle of class.

"Okay," he said.

I wanted to thank him, but I just nodded and took my seat.

Not only did Trip meet me at the library, he came early and helped me read to the kids and keep them all happy. I guess he could tell that I just wasn't myself. He put all the books back on the cart, and he spoke politely to Miss Homer while she turned the pages of a new book with a new long-haired man, hugging a new fainting lady, on the cover.

When we were done, I led Trip to these rooms in the back where people go for tutoring. It was always really quiet and private there.

I shut the door.

Looked at him.

I didn't know how to begin.

"Did you...did you ever think that something—that everything—was different than what you thought and that... someone you trust...is not telling you...something?" I knew I was babbling.

Trip twisted the key that hung around his neck. "What do you—what do you mean? Did you—what do you mean?" He looked scared. I'd probably look scared, too, if someone I thought was a normal human seventh grader suddenly started talking like a crazy person.

I took a breath.

And I said it fast.

"What if my mama isn't dead?"

Trip shook his head. "Wait, what?"

The tears I'd been holding back started falling and falling and falling as that giant tangled knot in my head started to come loose. Trip looked like he didn't know what to do. He began to reach out to me and then stopped.

"I found out something," I said between these big gulpy breaths.

"What do you—G, what did you find?"

"I found..." I looked up at his face. "I found Cherries in the Snow...." And then the whole story came tumbling out.

I told him about the lipstick, about Ida, about the list and the phone calls. I told him about Classic Cosmetics, the clickety keys, and 39 Red Cedar Road. I told him everything that had happened at Haven's house, and I talked and talked until the tangled-up knots in my head were all unraveled and lying there in a big messy heap.

"What are the chances that someone else in the whole wide world has Mama's and DiDi's exact name and wears Mama's lipstick and lives in our old town? What are the chances there's someone else in Verity—in the universe!— named Delta Dawn Barnes?"

"Did you talk to Haven and Allie about it?"

"No."

"Did you ask DiDi?"

My heart twisted. "No. You're the only person I've told. Trip . . . you're the only person I can tell."

Trip was quiet for a moment. Then nodded. Like he understood how there are some things you can only tell one person. He took my hand in his. It was the first time he had ever done that. "What are you going to do?"

I had been thinking about it every second of every moment since I'd heard Sales Associate Jamie say "39 Red Cedar Road." There was only one answer.

"I'm going to go."

Trip squeezed my hand. Hard. "What do you mean? Go

where? To that Cedar place? Like a million miles away? G, you don't even know if it's safe! You can't just go there all by yourself!"

"You're right," I said. "I can't."

And even though I knew it could make everything all tied up and tangled again, I pulled one last string.

"Trip, I need you to run away with me to South Carolina."

Tangled-Up Pie

- 1 tablespoon butter
- 1 tablespoon vegetable oil
- Leftover cold spaghetti with tomato sauce (about 4 cups)
- 2 beaten eggs
- 2 cups pizza cheese
- Crushed red pepper flakes and grated Parmesan cheese for serving

Now, I'll say right away that this works best with leftover spaghetti. I don't know why, but I'm guessing things are just better when they've had a chance to sit awhile and figure out what they want to be.

Heat up your best skillet and melt the butter with the oil in it. I like to get it up to medium-high heat, because then you get a nice crisp crust and the oil keeps the butter from burning right away.

Mix the cold spaghetti and eggs and cheese in a big bowl and then dump it into your hot pan. It'll sizzle right away and make the nice crust.

Lower the heat to medium and cover the skillet. After about 15 minutes or so, check it, and if it looks pretty good, slip a spatula in there and flip the whole thing over. Sometimes I slide the whole thing off onto a plate and then flip it over in the pan. Mary Elizabeth claims that if you practice a whole lot, you can flip it in the air, like those chefs in fancy restaurants. But I'll believe that when I see it. Let the other side cook and crisp up for maybe another 15 minutes, then when it's done, slide it onto a big plate and cut it into wedges. Pass the grated cheese and red pepper flakes.

Serves 4.

thirty-three

I had never run away before, but I knew that all I needed was a good plan.

Since I was little, DiDi has been telling me that a good plan is just like a good recipe. You find out what you need. You find out what to do. Then you follow the directions. I've been watching DiDi follow recipes since the day I was born, and you can bet I knew a good recipe when I saw one.

This was not a good recipe.

RECIPE FOR RUNNING AWAY TO FIND YOUR MAYBE NO LONGER DEAD MAMA

Friday night

- 1 Fake Sleepover with Haven and Allie (for me)
- 1 Fake Sleepover with Billy (for Trip)
- 1 "borrowed" credit card (Trip's dad's)
- "Borrowed" cash from the cookie jar where Trip's mom keeps grocery $ for the housekeeper
- My little stash of babysitting money
- Two tickets on the local Long Island train into New York City
- Then two tickets on the Overnight Express train from New York to South Carolina

First of all, give friends no information other than This Is Life or Death, Can I Fake Sleep Over at Your House?

Trip and I sneak out. (Haven and Allie and Billy turn all lights out early and stuff sleeping bags with pillows in case parents peek in on them.)

Next morning, they tell their parents we got sick and quietly went home, but DON'T CALL to check up on us, because we are probably sleeping and it would be rude to wake us up.

If possible, mention a High-Grade Fever. That's a fever of, like, 104 degrees or more. Parents lose their minds over a High-Grade Fever. DiDi will make me crawl to school with a sore throat and buckets of green stuff coming out of my nose, but if I have a High-Grade Fever, she'll let me sleep a week. Even my darn fever has to sound like it's on honor roll for DiDi to pay attention.

Keep all grown-ups from talking to each other till we get back.

Mix it all together.

Cross fingers. And just see what happens.

Like I said:

Not a good recipe.

But we only had that week to plan it, and it was the best we could do. We would sneak out of the house, and Trip would pay for a cab to get us to the local train that would take us to the big train station in the city—which for some reason was called Pennsylvania Station even though it was in New York. From there, we would have to transfer to another train and ride all night till we got to South Carolina. It was going to be expensive, but I had enough money saved for some of my ticket, and I promised Trip I would pay him back for the rest when I could.

The night of the Fake Sleepover at Haven's house, I peeked out the window about three hundred times. We were having the pretend sleepover downstairs in the TV room, so I'd be able to climb out a window close to the ground. Her parents had two other couples over, and they were laughing and talking in the dining room. Haven said it was called the Supper Club and they took turns having dinner at each other's houses. At first, I thought it'd be a bad idea to try the Fake Sleepover on Supper Club Night, but Haven said it was probably a good thing.

"Believe me, if they didn't have company over, my parents would try and hang out with us and make us do karaoke with them or something. But when their friends are over, they don't even peek in on me. It takes them like five hours to eat. They don't even have dessert till eleven. Plus, they put the Beast to bed early. Trust me, it's better this way."

I still didn't know the Beast's real name, since that's what Haven always called him. She had warned him to stay in his room and not bother us. Allie told him she would tell all the kids in kindergarten that he still wet his pants. Haven kidnapped his favorite army men and threatened to torture them. DiDi always says it's easier to make a friend than fight an enemy, so I snuck three forbidden slices of pizza to him after his lights were out. And so far, we hadn't seen him or Haven's parents since they dropped off the pizza cartons and plates in the TV room before their guests arrived. I hadn't eaten a bite.

"Where is he?" I whispered. "Where is he?"

"Leia, calm down," Haven said, chewing her fingernails. "He'll be here."

Meanwhile, Allie was pacing back and forth, twisting this old baby blanket of hers she called Banky. "I knew this wouldn't work. I bet the cops got him. I bet he got caught by the cops."

"The cops?" Haven said. "Seriously?"

Allie moaned and began tying poor Banky into a giant knot. Just like we planned, I hadn't told the girls what was really happening. Only that I needed to run away with Trip for a few days and it was Life or Death. Watching Allie torture Banky made me wish I could tell her the truth, but I doubted it would make things any better. I peeked out the window again. A cab pulled around the corner and parked behind the third tree on the sidewalk. That was the signal.

"He's here!" I started grabbing things, my backpack, my jacket, the cell phone Haven was lending me. "Okay, everyone stay calm. I'm just going to climb out the window like we rehearsed. I guess this is it."

Allie looked at me all tragically, then threw herself back on the sofa and pulled Banky over her head.

"Good luck!" said Haven, giving me a quick hug. She opened the window to let me out.

I put one leg over the sill. Trip was late. I wondered if we'd still have time to make the first train. I jumped out. Haven threw down my backpack and quickly closed the window and turned out all the lights. The plan was in effect.

Though I couldn't exactly appreciate it under the circumstances, Haven's house had the biggest and most beautiful yard I'd ever seen. It was filled with all these different kinds of gardens, with trees and plants that flowered no matter what season it was. She said her parents were gardening freaks and were up every weekend at the break of dawn, tending to their plants and waking her and the Beast up—sure that they wanted to share in the excitement of pulling weeds. The front yard alone had to be at least as big as the football field at school. In gym class, we get timed running across that field, and I knew it wouldn't be long until I was safe in that cab with Trip.

Luckily, there wasn't anything planted under the window where I landed. It was one of the few empty spaces on the property. The dirt was soft and I crouched there for a second while I settled my backpack onto my shoulders. The street was quiet and it was pretty dark, so even if people were out, they wouldn't necessarily see a twelve-year-old girl sprinting for her life across that big lawn. I took a deep breath and was about to make a run for it when a voice from around the corner whispered.

"I don't think this is a good idea."

I fell over and face-planted right in the dirt.

"Trust me, she loves surprises. Let me just show you this one empty spot under the window. It's perfect. Next summer, I'll grow my tomatoes there—"

One empty spot under the window? I scrambled on all fours as quickly as I could over to the next bush that would give me any sort of cover and curled up into a little ball behind it. "Tomatoes? You're going to plant tomatoes in your wife's rare-tree garden—"

"It's not her garden, it's our garden, and yes, she'll love it."

Suddenly, there were more voices. "What are you guys doing out here? The next course is up."

"Nothing."

"Nothing?"

"Not a thing."

"You're not talking about putting tomatoes in my last empty spot, are you?"

"Maybe."

Everyone started laughing.

"Not happening."

"Not just any tomatoes—rare heirloom tomatoes. Just come take a look...."

I could hear the sounds of Mr. Chang trying to drag Mrs. Chang toward me. I squeezed my eyes shut.

"And you really think it will help your cause to do this when I have food waiting?"

"Good point. Okay, but I promise, you'll love it. They'll be beautiful—just like you. Did you know the tomato is also known as the love apple?"

The grown-ups were laughing and it sounded like they were going to go back in. I had to hurry.

"C'mon!" I said to myself. I was going to have to make a run for it before Mr. Chang convinced his wife to come out and look at his dream tomato garden again.

Just like gym class, I thought to myself, standing up.

"Did you—Honey, what was that?"

I ducked back down. Dang it.

"That better not be the Millers' dog, leaving his little—Shoo!"

"I'll get him—"

I held my breath. This was it. I was a goner for sure.

"Mommy! Daddy!"

I looked up.

It was the Beast. Hollering from his bedroom window.

"What are you doing up this late?" Mrs. Chang yelled up. "And how did you open the childproof latch on that window?"

Oh, that Beast. He was grinning a wicked grin right down into my hiding place. Darn it. I should've wrung his neck. I should have threatened him with curses. I should have tied him up with old Banky.

"I—I'm scared! I want you and Daddy right now!"

"One moment, honey, I just have to—"

"RIGHT NOW!"

"Coming! Coming! Let's get in. Honestly, he'll keep this up all night—did you ever hear what Haven calls him?"

This time, I didn't move until I was sure I heard the door open and close. I exhaled and looked up at the window. The Beast waved at me as he chewed on the crust of his pizza.

I gave him a shaky thumbs-up. It was time.

I brushed the dirt off my legs and tried to wipe it off my face, mostly just smearing it around more. But that didn't matter. All that mattered was getting to Trip.

I took a big breath and ran for it.

Thudding one foot after the other.

Focusing on that taxi.

Trip would have already told the driver a story about how we were cousins and our aunt was going to meet us at the train station in the city. With his Wish Pie eyes and Perfect Boy manners, Trip would make everything okay.

I ran harder than I'd ever run in my life, aiming straight at that cab, each step taking me closer and closer and closer, till finally, gasping for air and pushing the hair off my dirty face, I grabbed at the door handle and hauled it open, throwing myself into the backseat. "Why in the world are you so—"

I stopped short.

But then, I guess the smile on Mace's face would be enough to stop anyone.

The Ol' Switcheroo

You think you're about to enjoy something warm and soft and comforting, straight from the oven, when WHAM! You sink your teeth into this icy brick of ice cream.

Friend, you've just been had by the Ol' Switcheroo.

- 4 egg whites
- A pinch of salt
- ¾ cup sugar
- 6 individual sponge cakes
- Vanilla ice cream

Take out your old electric beater and beat those egg whites with the salt till they start to make peaks. Add the sugar a few spoonfuls at a time till they make glossy stiff peaks.

Arrange the cakes on a parchment-covered cookie sheet. Scoop ice cream on top of each sponge cake. Spread meringue on top of each cake, covering the ice cream and cake and sealing it all the way down. Stick the cookie sheet in the freezer for at least an hour.

When you're ready to serve, pop the cakes into a 425°F oven for 5 minutes.

Just enough time to turn that meringue a beautiful golden brown but still keep that ice cream frozen. Serve right away!

Give it a try. It'll surprise your guests and it might even surprise you, too.

Serves 6.

thirty-four

ey, cuz!" Mace was smiling like we were best friends instead of I don't know what. "Sorry about being—What's on your face? Never mind. Listen, Aunt Joan said to look for her as soon as we get to the train station, so we better hurry, okay?"

Not only was Trip the only person I wanted to see right now, but Mace was also the last person I would ever want to have by my side when I was looking for my Maybe No Longer Dead Mama.

Mace mouthed, *Answer me*.

"Huh?" I said.

"You two are cousins?" The cabdriver was studying us in the rearview mirror. "You two..."

There was a second of silence.

Mace crossed her arms and smiled at the cabdriver. "Oh, she's adopted."

"Wha—" I started to say, but Mace shoved me in the ribs.

She went on. "We're meeting our aunt Joan at the station, and then we're all going into the city to a big family reunion. It's going to be great. Right, cuz?"

I tried again. "Aunt Jo—"

"Now, that's nice," said the cabbie, pulling out into the road. "Though I went to one of them family reunions once. Didn't care for it—I'll tell you why. My second cousin from my pop's side married this no-good stinking lunatic—a real loon, I tell ya—and this nutjob thinks since he's married into the family, he's got a right to my great-great-grandpop's wooden leg. Figured he could turn it into a lamp or somethin'...." As the cabdriver yakked on, Mace just kept looking straight ahead.

I turned away from her and stared out the window into the black night.

Where was Trip?

Why was Mace here?

It was like being handed the worst Mystery Basket in the history of Mystery Baskets. And, just like on the TV show, I had no choice. I had to see what I could make of it. But if Mace thought I wasn't going to come down hard on her the second we got out of that cab, she was wrong. She was dead wrong.

226

thirty-five

It was late and the station looked pretty much empty when we got there.

"Do not talk," Mace said in a low voice out of the corner of her mouth. "Thank you so much!" she said to the cabbie, handing him money. "And seriously, good luck getting back your great-great-grandfather's, um, leg-thing...."

"Now, that's awful nice of you to say. You kids have a nice family reunion. You see your auntie? I don't want to leave you here in the dark."

"Yes, there she is!" Mace pointed to a lone car, waiting with its lights on. "Hey, Aunt Joan!" She waved, then turned back and gave him a big tip.

More money! I started to protest. There was no way I

wanted to owe Mace anything. Anything. Especially when I still had no idea why she was even here with me in the first place. She didn't care about me. She didn't even know anything. About Mama or the lipstick.

Trip was the only one who knew the whole plan.

About being cousins and going to the train station.

Trip was the only one.

What If…

No. He would never tell Mace my secret. I didn't care how long they'd known each other. This much I knew.

Mace waved and waved at the cabbie, then grabbed my arm and began to drag me off across the sidewalk.

The second she put her hands on me, I found my words. I wrenched away from her. "I'm not going anywhere until you tell me what you're doing here. Where is Trip? And who is Aunt Joan?"

Mace blew the icy-blue piece of hair out of her eyes and glared at me. "Yeah, about that, Trip said you wanted to say Aunt Lori, but I thought maybe it would be cooler if she was named after Joan Jett. Of Joan Jett and the Blackhearts?"

"Black who? That's not what Trip and I—"

"Look, Trip asked me to come—no, wait, he begged me to come. Billy's mom caught him trying to climb out the window and called his mom and now he's grounded and Billy's grounded. He called me, freaking out."

I started to open my mouth, but she cut me off.

"I'm supposed to be with Chase and Laney at Laney's aunt's for the weekend. Shopping and having the best time, but I'm here with you. You. I had to lie to Chase and Laney and tell them I couldn't go, but my parents still think I'm going! I had to pretend the cab was Laney's aunt and run out before anyone saw." She leaned toward me till we were practically nose to nose. "Worst. Plan. Ever."

"But why—"

"Look, just let me finish. Trip and I have known each other since we were babies. Before you showed up and decided to take him all for yourself." She held her hand up to my face. "He called me. ME! Because Trip knows he can trust me more than anyone . . . and he knows how important DiDi is to me." The fire suddenly went out of her. She looked down.

How important DiDi was to her? To *her*?

"I don't need your help," I said.

"Really?" Mace took a step away from me. "You want to go by yourself? You have the money?" She reached into her jeans and pulled out a shiny gold credit card.

Of course. Trip was supposed to help me pay along the way, and I was going to pay him back. I didn't have enough money, and Mace did. Every darn kid in the school had a credit card in their back pocket but me. DiDi had a million dollars minus taxes in the bank, but I still didn't have enough to find Mama. I shut my eyes and turned away.

"Forget it," Mace said. "That was harsh. Let's just go."

I didn't know what to say. Our trip had hardly begun. The train was pulling in and we still had to get all the way into New York City, and I had no idea what I was doing. I had counted on Trip to get me there. Now all I had was Mace. And no choice.

thirty-six

It was late when we arrived at Pennsylvania Station, but it was packed with Friday-night travelers. As Mace made her way through the crowds, it made me think maybe that was the reason Trip picked her: She knew her way around. I mean, she was always going on and on about shows and shopping and museums. It couldn't be because Trip trusted her more than anyone else.

Mace bought our tickets to South Carolina and stood under this giant board that was hanging from the middle of the ceiling. It looked like it had about a hundred different trains with a hundred different names and a hundred different tracks and times. Northeast Corridor. Washington Express. Trenton Local. Track 10. Track 4. Track 16. But Mace just planted her feet, raised her chin, and gave her hair a toss. She'd probably done this a hundred times.

"Track number, track number..." I heard her saying to herself. She looked back toward the information booth, then up at the giant board. Then down at the tickets. That's when I noticed they were practically bent over double. And that her hands were shaking.

Then she saw me watching her and, just like that, her face snapped shut. "What? I've just never—I know my way around, okay? It's just—I usually have my mom or someone with me—but I know what I'm doing."

"Okay," I said.

"And can you please stop staring like you've never been in a decent city before? Just follow me. You still have dirt on your face."

She marched us into the ladies' room like she was going to declare war on it. Every other sink that lined the walls was clogged or broken. There was a woman in the corner dressed in rags and tatters, dragging a big black garbage bag. I don't know how she got it in there, because it was stuffed to the top with old clothes and newspapers and worn-out blankets that looked like Banky's long-lost cousins from the bad part of town. The smell coming from her was worse than the dump a few miles from my old school where the rough kids would go to smoke and who knows what else.

We did our business as quickly as possible, and even though I washed my hands and face twice, I still felt dirty when we left.

Mace went back and checked the big schedule board about ten more times. The tickets were sweaty and crumpled. Finally, they called our train. The Southeastern Overnight Express. We would travel all night and arrive really, really early the next morning. From there we would take a cab to Verity.

"Just try not to be noticed," Mace said under her breath. "Here, sit near that woman. The one with the good bag."

I watched Mace trail behind a well-dressed woman with the kind of bag that had somebody else's initials stamped all over it. We sat, clutching our backpacks to our laps. When the conductor came along, Mace suddenly started chatting into her cell in a loud voice. "Yes, Auntie—uh, we're just a few rows behind you! Thanks for letting us sit by ourselves."

The conductor didn't really seem to care. He just punched our tickets and moved on.

Mace took a deep breath, then pulled some headphones from around her neck and put them on. Without a word she turned her head away from me and closed her eyes.

Earlier, when the Long Island train had pulled into Pennsylvania Station, it had gone through this long tunnel. It was pitch black and the minute we were in, this terrible pressure began pushing into my ears. Even though I pressed my hands against them, it kept building and building with this low dull roar, till, finally, it released. I tensed, waiting for the same thing to happen again, but this big Southeastern Overnighter meant business and just shot out like a cannonball into the wide-open night. I didn't even get a chance to get used to the idea.

It wasn't until the speakers announced the name of the train again and all the stops in order that I relaxed. We had done it. Well, as much as I hated to admit it: Mace had done it. I peeked at her next to me, curled up in a ball, fists tight as knots, and I couldn't help it. I knew that tiny grudging nudge I felt inside me was gratitude.

I looked out the window and watched the night go flying by in all shapes and sizes, speckled with lights. It was late and I wondered if I would be able to sleep. How could I? Then I thought about how DiDi used to say to me, "Double G, you don't go thinking about the milk and eggs when you're still sifting the flour. Mama's recipe says when you make pancakes, the wet and dry stuff doesn't even get mixed together till the end, so why make yourself crazy? One thing at a time, baby girl. One thing at a time."

DiDi. Mama.

I shut my eyes to the rushing night outside the train window. The thought of Delta Dawn Barnes living somewhere hundreds of miles away, ordering Mama's lipstick, was something I could not even think about yet. I would take their advice and get through the train ride first. One thing at a time.

I guess I fell asleep, because the next thing I knew, the conductor was hollering for our stop and people were pulling their luggage down from the overhead racks.

Mace sat up, one headphone in and the other dangling out.

We grabbed our backpacks and worked our way off the train. The sun hadn't come up yet. It wasn't even close. It was cold and dark, and the stop was more spread out than I'd expected. Mace turned and waved at the conductor, who was still standing in the doorway.

"Thank you!" she yelled, pointing at her phone. "Our aunt said she'd be here in a minute!" The conductor nodded and waved back.

Our seats were at the far end of the train, and we had to walk down a ways to get to the station house. It was small and all the lights were off inside. There wasn't a cab in sight. As far as I could see, the buildings around us were dark for blocks. It looked like we had stopped in the middle of a ghost town. I could feel myself starting to panic. I moved closer to Mace, pressing against her, trying to shrink us down to nothing.

We stood there, trying our best to look like nothing more

than a couple of cousins, hanging around waiting for Aunt Whoever. The other passengers who got off at the same time seemed to know that this was the kind of station where you call ahead and have someone waiting for you.

Most of them were getting hugs from sleepy friends and family. Others were walking toward drivers holding up signs with their names. Mace and I looked at each other. If we didn't figure out something really fast, we were going to be left there alone in that dark empty place.

"Okay, okay. Let's just let me think." She scanned the parking lot, then grabbed my arm. "Quick, the lady with the bag, now!" she whispered.

We walked over as fast as we could.

"Hi!" Mace called to the lady. "We came from New York, too! Your bag is so cool. My mom has the same one, but she says I have to wait till my Sweet Sixteen." She was smiling and looking innocent as can be, even with that rock star haircut.

The woman was waiting while a driver put her luggage in the back of his car. "Why, thank you. I just got it. Are you girls okay? Do you have someone picking you up?"

"We're fine," answered Mace. "I mean, our aunt Joan is supposed to pick us up, but she just called to say she's having car trouble and she'll be a while. But it should be safe if we wait here for her. Don't you think? It should only be...an hour...or more...."

"An hour?" The woman looked around. "It's going to be pretty scary here in about ten minutes. Can I drop you off? Where is your aunt's?"

"Oh no," said Mace. "We don't want to trouble you. She's...she's staying at a hotel. One that's really close by. We could probably walk there." Mace turned to me. "What was the name of the hotel? It was really close—and nice. She said it was one of the really nice ones, right?"

I just stood there. She'd been telling me to hush up so much, I wasn't sure if I was supposed to answer or not. I settled for kind of grunting at her and giving this weird-looking shrug. Mace rolled her eyes and turned back to the woman.

"Anyway, we don't want to inconvenience you....I just wish I could remember the name...."

"Well, there's the South Bridge Suites if she said really nice. Right in downtown."

"Yes! South Bridge Suites! That's it. Thank you."

"Please let me drop you off," said the woman. "It's no trouble. I pass it on my way."

Mace pretended to think about it. "Well, if you're sure it's no trouble..." I never thought of Mace as all that appealing, but I guess she could do that Perfect Girl thing just as well as Trip did Perfect Boy. Yesterday, that thought would have upset me. Right now, nothing made me happier.

"No trouble at all. It would be my pleasure."

I sighed in relief as we climbed into the cab with her.

"So," said the woman, glancing back and forth between us. "You're, uh, cousins?"

Mace kept the conversation going for the next several minutes, while I just stared at my shoes. I was glad when the hotel came into view. It sure looked nice to me.

When we walked in, Mace went straight to the little desk with the clerk. I stayed quiet and listened to her fiddle up some tall tale. About how her mom was at our aunt's and wanted us to go ahead and book the room and what a pretty blouse the clerk was wearing. Next thing I knew, Mace was handing her a credit card and the clerk was handing Mace a key.

"Oh, we also need to know how to get to this address." Mace looked over at me. "What was Aunt Joan's address again?"

"Aunt—Oh! Thirty-Nine Red Cedar Road in Verity," I said.

The hotel clerk typed the address into her computer and said, "Red Cedar, Red Cedar... got it. Not a bad cab ride. It's hard to see, though. There's no sign or anything, just a small road that leads into the trailer park."

"Trailer p—" Mace coughed and looked down at the floor. "Well, it's not really our actual aunt. It's just a friend that we have to call Aunt to be polite."

I felt my face beginning to burn.

The hotel clerk handed her the map. "Well, here you go. Just call me if you want a cab."

Mace thanked her. When we got up to the room, she dropped her backpack and threw herself on one of the beds. "Thank God. Thank God. Thank God," she kept repeating. "Okay, we're safe. No offense, but it actually isn't as bad as I always thought the South would be."

DiDi says anytime a person starts a sentence with No Offense, you can bet they plan on saying something offensive. It didn't matter that Mace had gotten us here safe and sound. Nothing had changed. I was still just some hick she had to help out with her gold credit cards and fast thinking. I was tired and numb and just wanted to collapse. But I couldn't stop the words running through my head.

Delta Dawn.

Cherries in the Snow.

39 Red Cedar Road.

Verity.

What If.

thirty-seven

The hotel room was clean and neat and pretty. All shades of green and blue with striped covers on the beds and some kind of painting that I guess was supposed to be a river. Or a bridge. Or maybe a sandwich.

I went into the little bathroom and shut the door. I just needed a second to myself. I needed to be in a space where Mace didn't exist and I didn't have to look at her rock star haircut or breathe the same air she was breathing. I shrugged my backpack off, unzipped the little side pocket, and pulled out the KOB Trip had given me one hundred years ago on his hill. I had kept my promise. It was still folded. I tucked it deep and safe into the pocket of my jeans.

When I came out, Mace hadn't moved from the bed. I

didn't know how to handle all the things I couldn't help thinking around her. But I knew I could Say It Like It Is.

"Listen," I said. "I—I appreciate your help and especially getting around the city and all. I plan to pay you back every penny. Trip already knew I was going to pay him back. I work hard and I can babysit."

Mace sat up and shrugged. "It's not a big deal."

My face got hot. "Well, I'm sorry that money isn't a big deal to you, and maybe you wouldn't miss a couple hundred dollars, but for me and DiDi—"

"Defensive much?" said Mace. "I mean it's not a big deal and—you can pay me back whenever you want. I know how hard you work, okay? What do you think DiDi talks about half the time?"

"What—what do you mean?"

Mace looked down. "Nothing."

Then she turned away and got busy sorting her things.

She pulled out the map and began to study it.

I just stood there. And she just kept staring at the map.

"What's at that trailer park, anyway?" she finally asked. "What's on Red Cedar Road?"

I turned away.

Mace looked down at the map again. "Fine. Don't tell me." I could hear the crunch of the paper as she gripped it harder. "Why should I know?" she muttered. "I only got you all the way here and paid for everything and got us a room so

241

we wouldn't be murdered in the middle of the night at some random train station."

I didn't answer. I knew she had gotten me to the city. To the train. To this hotel. I knew how much she had done. And at that moment, it occurred to me that she was asking because Trip hadn't said a word to her about the details. She'd done it all without even knowing why. Or what it was about.

She knew nothing about Mama. Or Cherries in the Snow.

"Forget it. It's just—" She began studying the map again. "Forget it. Here, give me your phone."

I didn't know what to do for a second; then I fished Haven's phone out of my bag and handed it to her.

"I'll add my number just in case you—you screw up and need me to bail you out."

I watched as she busied herself setting up the phone for me.

When she was finished, she handed the phone back. "I guess you're ready."

I took it. And still didn't say anything. There was a long stretch of quiet.

And then it got a little longer.

Finally, Mace looked up at me. "Do you—do you want me to come wi—"

I shook my head.

She looked down again and got busy in her backpack. "Here." She pulled a bright-pink water bottle from her bag and held it out. I just stared at it.

"It has a filter, so you can drink water from anywhere and it won't be gross. My mom always says a body can handle just about anything as long as it's properly hydrated."

I took the water, because taking it just somehow felt like the only way I could actually give her something.

There was nothing more to say. She folded the map and handed it to me, then picked up the phone to call for a cab.

I held the map tightly.

Like it was filled with answers, and I didn't want a single one to escape.

thirty-eight

The cab was easy. Maybe it was too early, but the cabdriver wasn't super-talkative, so I didn't have to hear stories about wooden legs or crazy relations or anything. She just said, "Sure, I know the place. Real easy to pass. Unless you know what to look for, you'll never see it coming." Other than that, she stayed quiet. Truth is I could have used the distraction. I tapped my fingers against the window, until the cab took a sudden turn and pulled to a stop. It was just like she'd said: If you hadn't known it was there, you'd never have seen it coming. It was barely a road. Mostly dirt, with a crooked path leading into rough land that was part open and part small woods.

"What number did you say?"

"You can just drop me off at the entrance," I said, reaching for the money Mace had given me. I needed a minute to get my thoughts together. I didn't want to just pull right up to 39 Red Cedar Road in a big noisy cab, demanding to see my Not Dead Mama.

"Sure thing," said the taxi driver. She watched me for a second. "I'm just finishing up a shift, so I'll be visiting my girlfriend at the diner just a ways down the street. If I'm still around when you want a ride back, just look for me there. Okay?"

I had no idea how long I would be. Or even if I would just end up turning around and making a run for it. But I nodded and thanked her.

There were some sparse trees on either side of the entrance, and the road was rubble and dirt. But I was used to dirt roads and this was Verity. The place I was born. DiDi never wanted to talk about the details of where we lived before we moved to Lori's town—only that we'd left after Mama died and it made her too sad to think about it. I hated making DiDi sad, so I never asked. I peered down the twisty length of Red Cedar Road.

Was this it? If I looked long and hard enough, would I see the sooty remains of a long-ago fire? Had there ever even been a fire? And was Mama still here?

I thought of our old place in Lori's town. I thought about Davey Dylan and his nine fingers, out poking around for snappers. The neighbors coming over with cookies for no reason at all. No one would've looked down on DiDi's job there. Why, they would've thought it was amazing that she worked in such a beautiful place with big windows painted in curly black letters and a fancy sofa that everyone called a divan. Not to mention free chocolate chip cookies and coffee all day long.

Would Red Cedar Road feel the same?

Would it feel like coming home?

A few steps in let me know that this trailer park was nothing like our old one. No big strong sign. No nicely kept flower boxes in the windows. No whites hung up to dry in neat rows on laundry lines. No early-morning couples having coffee and reading the paper in folding chairs.

This was different. This was the kind of place that DiDi would prefer I didn't go.

Our old place had clean homes in neat rows on paved streets. The trailers here looked beaten down by life, and Red Cedar Road dipped and turned. I wasn't sure how the taxi driver would have figured out how to find Number 39 even if she had driven in.

I made my way along the path best I could, watching the numbers on the trailers as I walked by...3...6...9.

It was still pretty early. I didn't even know if anyone was up yet.

The path took a sharp turn into the trees.

12...15...18.

I realized I was humming the counting-by-threes song

the librarians at my old school used to sing...21...24...27...30.

I stumbled over a rock and caught myself before I fell on my face. The road looked like it went down a hill where there were a few scattered homes.

I didn't see Number 39 right away. It was set back on the wooded side of the property in this sort of shady area. The numbers were hammered into a tree in front.

I reached out to touch them and all the What Ifs I'd been keeping quiet inside me started to break out. What if there had been a mistake? What if Mama hadn't died in that fire? What if she had run away and knocked her head and woken up in some strange hospital not knowing her own name or even that she had children? I imagined Mama sitting alone and not knowing who she was. Needing us. Not knowing how much we needed her.

I could hear my breath turning harsh and raspy.

I tried to calm myself and slow it down. But it only got louder.

I tried holding it.

...But it still didn't stop.

Instead, it turned into a low growl.

Coming from the shadow beside me.

I saw the dripping, snarling teeth first. Flattened ears and low tail. Then yellow eyes, glaring.

A voice spoke.

"Oh, you're going to have to buck up a bit braver than that if you think you can get in here and steal from me, you little thief. Move one muscle and I'll set him on you."

Whoever was speaking didn't have to worry.

I couldn't move a muscle. I couldn't even breathe.

Thirty-Nine

What are you doing here and what do you want?"

"I—I'm looking for my—I'm looking for Delta Dawn Barnes, sir. I'm not a thief—I swear."

"Delta what? No one here by that name. Don't make me show you what Lucifer does when he's hungry." The growling from the shadow grew even louder.

"Thirty-Nine—she's supposed to be at Number Thirty-Nine Red Cedar Road." My legs shook like dead leaves on a tree. I turned my eyes toward the voice. All I could see was shadow and shirtsleeve.

"Thirty-Nine? You mean Miss Dawna?" The dog was still growling, all low and mean, but now he was down on the ground. Lying there as if to say, *Oh, I can leap up and kill you in about a second. I just want to rest for a bit.* "Three doors down. I believe you best be going."

I turned and stumbled back to the main path.

It wasn't until I got to the tree with the house number on it that I knew I was breathing again. I looked up and saw that I had been at Number 36 with the 6 flipped upside down from being on a broken nail.

I sank down onto the ground by the road, my heart pounding, waiting for the mess in my head to start making sense again. I reached into my backpack and took out the pink water bottle that Mace had given me. I couldn't remember the last time I had something to drink. To eat. I felt weak and empty. And walking from Number 36 to Number 39 suddenly seemed impossible.

As I sat there, I heard the sudden crunch of gravel. A pale-blue car pulled up and the front window went down. A woman peeked out and called, "You must be lost, baby girl, because I don't remember you and I think I know just about everyone around here. Can I help you find someone?"

I made myself get up, brushed off my jeans, and went toward the car.

"Hi," I said. "I'm looking for—"

DiDi was in the car.

And that was the last thing I remembered before everything went black.

forty

"Dang. It's kind of early in the morning for drama, don't you think? C'mon now. Be a nice little girl and get on up."

Someone was giving me little slaps around the face. Then shaking me. Kind of hard. I didn't understand why. And then I remembered the yellow-eyed dog. And DiDi.

I opened my eyes. I was still on the ground. The blue car was parked next to me, and this woman was bending over me. She snapped her fingers a few times.

"Are you—" I tried to get up too quickly and my head spun again.

"Whoa there! Take it easy. I think you better come along with me. We'll get you where you need to go."

Her face looked exactly like an older version of DiDi's,

down to the little tilted point of her nose. And the pretty curve of her lip.

Mama.

"Let's get you into the car. My place is right up here, but it won't do anyone any good to have you fainting again."

As she leaned over to support me, something about her reminded me of Lori. Lori on those late party nights when I'd have to babysit her.

She helped me into her car and drove up to a trailer that looked like maybe once upon a time it was really pretty. And now just hanging on to the last bits of pretty.

Out front, a chippy blue mailbox was hammered to a tree with a little stuffed teddy held on with a faded ribbon. It was wearing a T-shirt that said KEEP OUT! THIS BEAR GIVES HUGS! I thought of that nice drugstore clerk, Ida, and her little pink KEEP OUT sign. That day seemed like a million years ago. And a million miles away.

Mama parked the car and came around to the passenger side. "Come on in now. I can't promise it's clean, but..." She opened the front door. "Not so bad now, is it? Can you stand on your own?" When I nodded, she let go of me.

I couldn't help staring as she made her way to the kitchen, slipping off her coat and tossing it onto a faded sofa. I waited for her to look at me twice. For some kind of small piece of recognition to show in her face. "I'm making you a cup of coffee—lots of sugar and creamer." She looked me up and down. "You know, you sure do stare a lot, baby girl. But then"—she did a little shimmy—"everyone stares at me."

As soon as she had coffee brewing, she reached into a cabinet and pulled out a bottle, and it didn't take a genius to see that it wasn't coffee she was pouring into her own mug. She took a big gulp, and as she drank, she looked nothing like DiDi.

She picked up a pack of long skinny cigarettes and offered one to me.

"No?" She laughed and lit one for herself. "Might as well start now. I did when I was about your age. Now tell me, what are you doing wandering around and fainting in the middle of the street?" She sat down on one of the two chairs and nodded that I should take the other.

A tiny ragged dog came padding up to her. She shoved it away with one high-heeled foot. It came back and she shoved it again. Hard.

I gasped and then coughed to cover it up. I didn't know what to say. How to begin.

"I..." I looked around the room, searching for an answer.

"Okay, take it easy. Let me get your coffee so you can get your mind back together." She toasted the air with her mug. "While I work on getting my mind back together."

As she fixed my coffee, she glanced at my backpack. "So what are you doing, some kind of school report or something?"

My mind started working. "Yes, I'm—I'm—interviewing people—for a paper on—the Truth."

"The Truth? What the heck kind of school paper is that?"

"It's a paper on the truth about—" I blinked and looked up. "Names."

"Names?"

"Yes, on the meaning behind names and—what people like to name their—their children. Stuff like that."

She handed me my mug and sat down. "If you want to know about names, I got a few stories. You're going to want to write this down."

I knew my school assignment book was in the front pocket of my backpack. I found a pen and quickly pulled it out. "I'll just need some, um, information. What's your full name, please?"

"Delta Dawn Barnes."

I pressed down hard with the pen to keep my hand from shaking. It ripped through the paper. "Sorry—sorry, let me—" I tore that piece out and started again. It was true. It was true. Mama was alive. Mama was alive and right here in front of me. "And—and what do you do for a living?"

She gave her curls a little pat. "You are looking at the best darn hairdresser in town. They line up for me day and night." She took a long drag of her cigarette. "Or used to, anyway. Just hard times now. But the fellows still line up to buy me drinks. That's worth something." She winked at me and exhaled.

My mind raced for what to say next. "Did you—did you always want to be a hairdresser or—"

"Honey, it's the only thing I was ever good at. It's not like I was a whiz at school. Hightailed it out of there after eighth grade. Hey, I thought this was supposed to be about names, not some fancy high school diploma."

I found myself reaching for the star on my forehead.

It was still there. It was real. But at that moment, nothing else seemed to be.

Mama was here and alive, but she was not the Mama I'd been told about. Not the Mama I'd dreamed of.

Not a scientist.

Not a brain.

Not like me.

Nothing like me.

Or was I the one who was nothing like I was supposed to be?

forty-one

lifted the mug of coffee with an unsteady hand and took a sip. It was sickly sweet. "Can you—can you tell me about your name?"

"Now that, little girl, is an interesting story." Mama inspected the tip of her cigarette. "Delta Dawn was a top ten song on the country music charts the month I was born. Recorded by this little thirteen-year-old girl. Thirteen years old. My mama showed her to me on the TV once. Singing there in her little tangerine dress and golden heels. That song changed her life." Even though she still had half the cigarette to smoke, she stubbed it out. "Guess it changed mine, too."

"What do you mean?"

"Well, as far as I see it, when someone gives you a name,

they are pretty much telling you what your life is going to be. You understand?"

I shook my head.

"Sit back, I'm going to give you a treat. . . ." She refilled her mug and then sort of sashayed over to this old record player. I remembered Lori having one like it.

"This, baby girl, is a forty-five," she said, holding up a little black record. "I don't know why they call it that. Sounds more like a gun, if you ask me." She pointed gun fingers at me. Bang. "It was my mama's. Kept it all these years."

She placed the record carefully on the turntable and then lifted the needle and set it down. I knew the song before it even started playing.

The twangy sadness of the voice.

The story that would never have a happy ending.

About a woman deceived and left behind by the man she loved.

Mama cranked up the volume and then sang along, howling out the high notes best she could. "That's the song I was named after. And what do you know? My life *was* ruined by a man." She downed the rest of what was in her mug and wiped her mouth. Her voice was starting to slur. "Come to think of it, there may have been more than one!" She shoved me in the shoulder and laughed. "And it's not like they left me anything worth keeping."

Mama pointed a chipped fingernail at me. "You. Girl.

257

Write this down word for word. My mama named me after this song. She's the one who handed me the life I have. This"—she gestured around the run-down trailer—"my life wasn't always like this. It's all my mama's mistake... giving me this name. Only mistake I ever made was passing it on to that worthless, no-good girl...."

DiDi. Was she talking about DiDi?

"What do you mean?"

"I mean passing on this name so she could end up somewhere just like this. Probably worse."

I thought of the nice trailer where I grew up that was always neat and clean. Of DiDi working in the prettiest salon I'd ever seen. Of her finding us a place to live across the street from a candy store.

I shook my head. "No."

Mama had made her way into the kitchen. "You say something? I think I got some leftover Chinese in here if you're hungry. Had a hot date a couple nights ago. Pretty sure it didn't go bad." She turned and looked at me over her shoulder. "The food, I mean. The date for sure was a bad one."

I looked around the tiny kitchen. "Do you—cook?"

Mama stopped and leaned against the counter. She rubbed her head and looked at her hands. "Well... I used to. Used to be darn good. Just... can't find my recipes anymore...."

My heart gave a twinge of guilt. I knew where her recipes were. At home with DiDi. And here Mama was—all alone.

Maybe that was why she was sad and drinking and lost. I was gone and DiDi was gone and her recipes were gone. That would be enough to change anyone. Maybe we could've stayed and helped her the way I helped Lori when she had One Too Many. I was good at it.

Mama shook herself and went over to the fridge. She pulled out a nasty-looking carton of food. "Anyway, good riddance, I say." She looked over at me as she tossed it into the garbage. "Way of the world. You have to get rid of trash before it turns on you."

"Turns—?"

"Turns on you." Mama began counting on her fingers. "Steals your money, your car, your brand-new purple pocketbook—with all your tips!—and takes off in the middle of the night. Just takes off—here, look at this." She pulled up her skirt and rubbed a big ugly scar that ran down her knee like jagged white lightning. "Chased after her down the street till I tripped.... Stole everything from me...everything I had...everything." She started muttering words I was not supposed to hear.

Everything. What did she mean, DiDi stole...everything?

Mama stumbled into the bathroom. I could hear her rattling around and dropping things.

"Hey, wanna hear something funny?" She came out holding a small plain cardboard box, shaking it. "Used to scare the living daylights out of that worthless fool who manages this place—thought it was full of shells."

My head was spinning. "Shells? Seashells?"

"Shotgun shells."

Mama took the lid off and I looked inside. A dozen golden tubes of lipstick rolled around. "He heard some rumor about me buying golden bullets. 'Course he was dead drunk, but maybe that's just something we have in common...."

And then I knew.

I didn't want to say it even to myself, because I didn't want it to be true. But I was already talking.

"The—the man who lives at Thirty-Six?"

"Merle, ya mean? Ol' Merle and his dog."

"He called you Dawna."

Mama shrugged. "Friends call me Dawna, and if Merle and that old mutt can keep the riffraff away from here, then I guess he's a friend."

The golden bullets...Mama howling her song...even the bear outside tied to the tree. Some of the things were just rumors grown ugly. Others were ugly because they were true.

"Getting tired of this conversation...." Mama stumbled over to the worn old sofa and laid herself down.

She was drunk.

She was drunker than drunk.

She was Dead Drunk Donna, and there was nothing I could do to change it.

"Time for you...go...."

"Wait." I couldn't leave yet. I had to ask her one last

question. I didn't care if she wondered how I knew to ask it. I needed to ask before she was too far gone to answer. "Are you...awake?"

Mama's eyes were closed. "Mmmm."

"You said...she stole...everything...." I leaned in close and lowered my voice. "Did you chase her because you wanted back your—did she—did she steal your baby?"

Mama breathed into the sofa.

"Mama?" I whispered. But she was dead asleep.

I sat by her side for a bit. Reached out and smoothed her hair. I looked around for a blanket to cover her shoulders and a pillow to tuck under her head. I found some aspirin and filled a glass with water and left them on the side table where she would see them when she woke up. I knew exactly what to do. After all, I had been babysitting for years.

I stared at her a long, long time.

Then, finally, I picked up my backpack and made my way out. Step by crooked step. Through the twisty paths and stumbling rocks. All the way back to that tricky entrance where you had to know what to look for or you'd never see it coming.

forty-two

shook my head at Mace when she opened the door.

She didn't say a word or ask me anything. I had never been so grateful to anyone in my life. She watched as I dropped my backpack and climbed into bed, pulling the covers over my head. I reached into my pocket so I could hold on to Trip's KOB. A few seconds later, I felt Mace carefully lifting the blanket and pulling my sneakers off. When she was done, she turned down the lights and closed the shades. It was dark and I couldn't see, but after a minute, I heard something that sounded an awful lot like a pink water bottle with its very own filter being filled and placed on the nightstand by my side.

I guess I slept through the rest of the day and the whole night. Mace gently shook me the next morning. She gathered our things and got me out to the waiting cab.

I stayed silent the whole train ride back, but Mace babbled at every grown-up who even glanced our way. Yakking on about cousins and waiting aunts. Cheerfully announcing that everyone should probably give us some space, seeing as I most likely had a High-Grade Fever. It worked. People stayed away. I kept my cheek pressed against the cool train window and stared at the passing world. Haven's phone blinked with about a hundred billion messages on it. I put it away without listening.

Mace forced me to take tiny sips from that pink water bottle. She handed me bits of a protein bar that she assured me was 100% organic with no artificial colors or flavors.

By the time we were home, it was night again, the day lost in travel and weariness. Mace paid for the cab that took us from the train station back to the apartment. "Do you need help getting up the stairs? Do you—do you need anything?"

I just shook my head.

I wanted to thank her for not making me talk.

For not asking questions.

For not needing to know.

But I just looked at her and hoped she knew what I was trying to say. I think she did. Anyway, I was surprised at how worried and sad her dark eyes looked.

forty-three

The second that old step at the top of the stairs creaked, I heard footsteps, running. Then DiDi was there, tearing the door open and grabbing me and pulling me into a fierce hug.

"Oh my God, GiGi—GIGI! Don't ever do that again! I have never been so scared! Haven's mom called—and the girls didn't know—then something about you and—and Life or Death—G! Where on earth did you—"

DiDi dragged me into the apartment and shut the door. Then she grabbed my face and just stared at me like a crazy lady. Curls coming loose from her bun. Dark circles under her eyes. Makeup smudged. She looked exactly like Mama at that moment.

I yanked myself out of her grip. "Thirty-Nine Red Cedar Road! Is there anything you want to tell me about Thirty-Nine Red Cedar Road, DiDi?"

DiDi's hands flew to her face. "What did she—she—?"

"She! Mama, you mean? The Mama I missed my whole life? The Mama I knew wasn't dead? The Mama"—I bit back a sob—"the Mama I needed? Who needed me?" I pushed the tears off my face. "Why did you tell me she was dead? Why didn't you tell me the truth?"

"The truth?" DiDi was shaking her head, her face twisted. "The truth? She was—she was a drunk—"

"Yeah, Dead Drunk Dawna."

DiDi shrank back at the name.

"Did you ever think of telling me that all those stories were about our mama?"

"Our—I—I was trying to protect you! She would've hurt you—"

"She needed me and you took me away from her. I could've taken care of her! Remember all those times I took care of Lori? She needed us and you ruined everything. She said you stole her money and car—and me—you stole me—"

"You—no! It wasn't like that, GiGi—listen. Please. After you were born, she changed. She wasn't the same Mama—not anymore. She started drinking all the time. She'd shake you whenever you cried. She couldn't deal. I knew I had to get you out of there—and then one day—one day, you were crying and crying and—just like that—she said it was too much and she...she pushed you."

DiDi reached out toward the star on my forehead.

My star.

The star that Trip said didn't look like any birthmark he'd ever seen before.

Birthmarks were brown blotches.

...But scars were white.

Jagged white.

Like lightning across a knee.

No. I shook my head.

It couldn't be true.

Just like that, it was too much. And she pushed me.

Then I remembered the dog. That poor little dog she'd shoved away without a glance.

"We had to leave," DiDi whispered. "I had to keep you safe."

I couldn't hear any more. I turned away.

"Baby—" DiDi began, but I held up my hand.

"My whole life . . . I wanted Mama," I said without turning around.

"I tried to give you what you needed."

I went into my room and locked the door. Then, for the second time in two days, I climbed into bed and fell asleep holding on to a worn, still-folded KOB.

forty-four

I woke up thirsty and hungry and not knowing what time it was.

Why I was still in my jacket.

And wearing sneakers in bed.

I looked out the window. It was quiet, with none of the usual traffic along Main Street. No sound. No moon. Not even a single star in the sky. I didn't know how many hours it was before morning. If the sun ever came up again. I opened my door and tiptoed into the kitchen. I filled a glass with water and drank it down. And another. When I was done, I let myself remember I had found Mama.

DiDi was on the sofa bed, her eyebrows all wrinkled up and worried, even in sleep. Blankets tumbled and twisted around her. I reached up and touched the white star on my head. Had there ever been even the littlest piece of time when Mama loved me? Just a bit?

Suddenly, I was desperate. I needed something. Some piece of proof. I needed to know that at some point, at some time in my life, Mama had loved me. DiDi had hidden the truth from me all these years. What else had she hidden? Maybe somewhere there was a photo or a letter or a diary or something. Something from when Mama first had me, before she started drinking too much. Before she got so sad and mean.

I went over to the double closet that DiDi and I shared and pulled it open. There were boxes of old things on the top shelf that DiDi never let me go through. She handled all the house stuff and organizing. She said she had a system and I should spend my time on the stuff that I was good at and she'd do hers. Boxes and boxes of papers and photos and such.

They were stacked in piles four and five high. I grabbed the chair from my desk and pulled it over. Half of the boxes held old school papers. I looked through them, amazed. DiDi had saved every piece of work I'd ever done in school. Every report card. Every spelling quiz. Every 100%. Every A+. Stacks and stacks filed neatly away like recipes she might need in case she ever had to cook up a feast to show the world I was going to be something.

Preschool. Kindergarten. First grade. Second. Third.

Fourth. Fifth. Sixth. Class photos. Notes from teachers, all glowing and bragging about me and my potential.

And then, way in the back, an old plastic bag, folded over and taped up.

I grabbed it.

There was something inside. I ripped it open. A pocketbook made of some kind of cheap purple leather.

The pocketbook DiDi had stolen from Mama.

Recipe to Lose 10 Pounds

Just don't open that fridge.

forty-five

Mama's pocketbook.

My mama's pocketbook.

I opened it carefully, like maybe the air trapped inside was still breathing with a whisper of her love for me. But it smelled stale. Inside was a wallet. Gas credit card. A couple of receipts. And an old driver's license. I looked at the picture of Mama on that license, which gave me more information about her than I'd ever had in my whole life.

She smiled too big in photos.

Her hair had once been dyed red.

Her birthday was April 25.

Such a pretty date. Nothing like the cold, wintry November dates of DiDi's and my birthdays. I liked the sound of it.

April 25. I wondered if she had birthday parties in the spring when she was little. Something else was rolling and rattling around the bottom of the pocketbook. I reached in and pulled out an old envelope. Underneath it was a faded gold tube. As I slowly twisted it open, a whole dried-out pinky-red lipstick rose up.

Now the tears came. A lifetime of wishing for Cherries in the Snow, and here DiDi had a tube all along. And was probably trying to forget about it.

I pulled a piece of paper from the envelope. DiDi's birth certificate.

And that was it.

All that she took to start our new lives together. Stolen money, now long gone, an old lipstick, and proof from the Verity Hospital of the day she was born.

The top of the closet was empty. There was nothing left of Mama for me to find.

I sat there, exhausted and numb.

I touched the star on my forehead.

But it wasn't a star anymore. It was just a scar.

I put the lipstick back and picked up DiDi's birth certificate.

Delta Dawn.

I tried to imagine DiDi as a baby. Had Mama ever loved her, either? Or had we both been born into a sad, sad life? Not wanted by anyone?

Delta Dawn.

Typed on the form, all crooked and careless. Names and dates not even lined up in their proper places. I pictured a pretty nurse on some old-fashioned typewriter, rolling her eyes and just trying to get the job done as quickly as possible. I touched each crooked word with the tip of my finger.

Father's name: [Unknown]

I made a face.

Mother's name: Delta Dawn Barnes

Child's name: Delta Dawn Barnes

I leaned in closer. The ink was all smudgy and under MOTHER'S NAME, it kind of looked like it said Delta Dawn Barnes II. And under CHILD'S NAME, it looked like Delta Dawn Barnes III.

Which didn't make any sense, because Mama was the first Delta Dawn.

And DiDi was the second.

I shook my head. That snotty nurse in her fancy white uniform—being all careless and not giving a darn about other people's important life documents. Why, she had even typed the wrong day for baby DiDi's birthday. She had typed... mine.

I blinked and looked again.

Some kind of voice in my head was warning me to stop.

But I didn't listen.

I looked at that birth certificate and I read it.

Again.

And again.

But no matter how many times I read, it didn't change the fact that the baby named Delta Dawn III was born on my birthday, in my birth year.

And the mother named Delta Dawn II was born on DiDi's birthday—but with a year that was not nine years away from mine. It was a good six years older than DiDi was supposed to be.

And then I couldn't think and I couldn't breathe, and the pressure in my ears began building and building till my head filled with the roar of a train heading into a tunnel where there was no coming back—a tunnel of screaming voices going faster and faster—until I realized the screaming was not in my head anymore. It was filling the room and it was coming from me. But I couldn't stop.

Not when DiDi came crashing in, tousled and wild-eyed.

Not when I pushed her away, kicking and hitting.

And not when I threw that crumpled piece of paper from the Verity Hospital at her, knowing that what I was really throwing at her was the truth.

It was not DiDi's birth certificate.

It was mine.

forty-six

hat is this? Who is Delta Dawn the Third? Why does she have my birthday? Why does her mother have yours? What is happening? Say It Like It Is, DiDi! Tell me the truth!"

DiDi was sobbing and gasping and trying to hold on to me. "There was a boy—I got pregnant—he disappeared—I never saw him again. Mama went crazy. When you were born, she forced me to name you after her and me—and she was drinking so much and I was afraid you would get hurt—I ran away with you. I had to—"

"No!" I cried. "You're lying!" I pointed at the crumpled paper. "That is a fake and it's not true—it can't be true and you can't be—"

"I wanted you to have your own life," DiDi said, sounding

like she was begging me. "I wanted you to have something I never had—"

"And you thought lying to me about who I was and what my name—" My heart dropped. "Who is Galileo Galilei?"

DiDi went pale. "Lori dated a textbook salesman who knew a little bit about science, and he told me about the name Galileo—"

"One of—one of Lori's salesmen named me—"

"I wanted to give you a name that showed what I thought you could be—I wanted to give you something—"

I held a hand up, cutting her off. "I don't want anything from you."

I tore away from DiDi's grasping hands. Shutting my ears to her voice calling me back. I pushed through the door. Down the stairs. And into the night and a world where I didn't know who I was.

forty-seven

I don't know how long it took me to walk to Trip's house.

An hour. A day. A month.

I didn't feel the cold. I didn't feel the night. I didn't feel anything. I stayed off the roads, and if a car went by, I slipped behind a tree. I didn't want to be seen. I didn't want to be found. Besides, if anyone found me, how would they know who they'd found? When I didn't even know who I was?

It was still dark and the whole house was quiet. I threw a pebble at Trip's window. And another. After a few tries, I saw his face appear for a second and I knew he was coming to get me. I ran to the back door.

He opened it, looking around, and beckoned me in. "G!" he whispered. "Hurry, get in! What are you doing here? Have you seen DiDi? She called yesterday and she's freaking out! My parents are having a heart attack. I told them I didn't know where you were. But then when everyone said they didn't know, DiDi thought you must have been kidnapped." He pulled me in. "Are you okay?"

He took one look at my face and knew the answer.

He kept one arm around me as we made our way up the stairs to his room and shut the door. I fell onto his bed, shaking and sobbing.

"G-Girl. Leia. Please. What happened?"

I shook my head into the pillow. "Don't say those names. I'm not Leia. I'm not G—I'm not even Galileo Galilei. I'm no one."

"What do you mean? What can I do?" He kept saying it over and over. And then I was up and sobbing into his shoulder, and he was holding on to me, and before I could stop myself, I was Saying It Like It Is. Spilling out every terrible, ugly detail. From the train station. To that yellow-eyed dog. Fainting. Mama in the car. Dead Drunk Dawna. The birth certificate.

And finally, the truth about DiDi. And me.

When I was done, I felt empty. But almost—almost a good empty. Like a thousand germs had left my body. I wiped the tears off my face with my hands and then wiped my runny nose on my sleeve from my elbow to my wrist and back again, which was just so nasty, I had to' laugh in this horrible, exhausted kind of way. Which made Trip laugh, too.

Though his eyes looked more like he was crying. He went into his bathroom and came back with a box of tissues.

"You know the funniest thing out of all this?" I said, blowing my nose.

"Something's funny?"

"It means I'm a Triple, too. I'm a Third. Just like you."

But Trip was the third in a rich family on the shore of a beautiful harbor, and I was named after an old country song about a crazy woman let down by a man. And what my life was meant to be felt like a wide and permanent road laid out before me, and DiDi playing the name game wasn't going to change any of it.

"It doesn't matter, G. I don't care—I just—" He grabbed my hands and squeezed them hard.

I looked into those eyes and my heart felt ready to burst. Here, Trip had heard every possible horrible, ugly thing he could've heard about anyone, and he was still holding on to me and letting me know it didn't matter. Not to him.

I wanted to have something pure and perfect in the middle of this nightmare.

So I closed my eyes to this terrible, terrible day and night and week.

And I kissed him.

The Perfect Kiss

If this is your first time doing this, I have to tell you everyone wants the perfect kiss.

Sweet, light, and melting on your lips. But truth is, you're just going to have to wait till you open that oven door to find how everything turns out.

- 4 large egg whites, at room temperature
- ½ teaspoon cream of tartar
- 1 cup superfine sugar

Preheat your oven to 225°F. Now, beat those egg whites with an electric beater till they're all nice and foamy.

Add the cream of tartar and beat some more.

When your egg whites are starting to stand a little on their own, little by little add the sugar, beating till that meringue is as stiff as a board and shiny as Christmas Day.

Put parchment paper on two cookie sheets. Drop teaspoons of the meringue an inch apart. Then use a knife to give the top a little swirl.

Place both sheets in the oven for 45 minutes.

Then shut that oven off and leave them there for an hour. Do not open the oven or even give them one little peek. That's the hardest part. But I've got my fingers crossed that everything will turn out just the way you want.

Makes 40 cookies.

forty-eight

Earlier in the school year, Trip had dragged a whole bunch of us to this horror movie festival. It was crowded and we all had to split up, so Trip made me sit with him in the front row. There were only two seats left, so it was just him and me. But as much as I wanted to sit alone with him at the movies, I wasn't exactly thrilled. I am not a fan of blood and guts and all, and I told him I couldn't even watch horror movies from the back row, blindfolded and wearing a potato sack. He laughed and said I just had to trust him.

So there we were, looking way up at that big screen, just waiting for this werewolf zombie to jump out of nowhere and rip the heck out of someone the way things do in the movies.

I had both hands over my eyes.

"Okay, listen," Trip said. "Hear that music? Classic Something Really Bad Is About to Happen Music. So, G—stop. It'll be okay. When I say, just turn around and look behind us—*now!*"

And without even really understanding what he was saying, I whipped my head around and saw the entire audience behind us, screaming and reeling back in horror. It was probably the funniest thing I'd ever seen in my life. This one guy, who was all big and brawny in a muscle shirt, made this high-pitched shriek and threw his soda all over his date. She started yelling at him and stormed out. He followed, bumping into people and apologizing and swearing that it hadn't been him squealing like a little girl—that it'd been someone else.

But Trip and I had seen the whole thing. That big muscle-y boy had practically cried like a baby. I grinned at Trip and he grinned back. And even though there were blood and guts flying everywhere, we were together and we had popcorn and candy, and the movie wasn't scary anymore, and, just then, that moment was perfect. A pure and perfect moment in the middle of the nightmare.

Kissing Trip was exactly like that.

Just not the perfect part. Our lips touched for about one millionth of one second, and, suddenly, there was nothing but air. I opened my eyes.

And the way he was reeling away from me with that look of horror on his face, you'd think he was watching the highlight film of every werewolf zombie movie ever made.

forty-nine

My cheeks went hot. I scrambled up and started for the other side of the room.

"Wait—" Trip said. "G, please wait—"

I couldn't think. I was tired and hurt. And mad. Madder than I'd ever been in my life. I spun to face him.

"What, you can kiss Mace and not me?" My voice cracked, which made me even madder.

"I never—"

"You did—Allie said you did in Spin the Bottle last summer."

"That didn't count. It was just a stupid—"

"You like her better—"

"I don't—"

"You do, and you abandoned me when I needed you and made me go to South Carolina with her—her of all people!"

"But I didn't—"

"And I am so sorry I'm not wrapped up like a perfect little cookie with your moms who are neighbors and best friends and—"

"No! Mace and I grew up together, but—but you're my best friend, G. And I'm sorry—but I don't like you—like that—"

"Why? Because I'm some dumb hick? And you are Perfect Boy? Mr. Trip Something-Something Hedgeclipper the Fourteenth? Because I'm trash? My whole family is trash all the way down to the very first Delta Dawn caveman!" I was yelling now and I didn't care who heard me.

"That's not it, G—"

"Then what?"

"It's just that I—"

"What?"

"I don't—"

"WHAT!"

"I don't"—his voice broke—"like *any* girl that way."

There was quiet. And breathing. But nothing in the quiet made sense.

I shook my head.

"What are you saying?"

"I think—no—G, I *know*—"

"What does that even mean? What do you mean *you know*?"

"I—I know this about myself, G—I know what I know."

I shook my head again.

He reached out, but I pulled away.

And I couldn't stop shaking. Shaking and shaking my head at him, sitting there telling me he knew what he knew when everything—everything!—in my whole life that I thought I knew was a lie.

I jumped up. "Do you want to know what I know? I move here and you keep hanging around and inviting me over, passing me notes and making me—making me foolish and stupid enough to believe that you—and then tonight, after—after everything—"

Then, just like that, it was too much.

And I pushed him.

Because if I was the direct descendant of Dead Drunk Donna, I was going to do it 150%.

Like I do everything.

I turned and ran out of the room.

Past the wall of laughing photos. Past the hundreds of books on his shelves. Past his mother and father standing there wordless in the unlocked doorway.

Heartbreak on Toast

When your heart's broken, you find comfort where you can.

- The best slice of bread in the room
- Butter
- 1 nice big egg
- Salt and pepper
- Hot sauce

Just go on and put your pan over medium-high heat and let it warm up.

Take a nice, clean little heart cookie cutter and use it to make a perfect heart in the middle of your bread. Butter both sides of your bread (and the little heart).

Drop both pieces into your pan and let it sizzle there until they are nice and golden brown and crisp on one side. Then flip them both over and crack your egg right in that hole. Cook until the white is set but the yolk is still runny. Flip it once more, just to set the other side. Put it on a plate. Salt and pepper. Poke a little hole in the yolk and hit it up with a dash or two of hot sauce. Use your crispy little bread heart to dip and eat. Dip and eat. Warm, buttery, toasty bread and egg. Just keep eating and eating till that heart-shaped hole is long gone.

Serves 1.

fifty

It wasn't a far walk from Trip's.

And it wasn't a hard house to find.

Billy had once told me it was the only house on the block that looked like it would still be standing after an earthquake. And seeing as I had pretty much survived a natural disaster of my own, I figured we had that in common and me dropping by way too early in the morning might be okay.

Mace opened the door and peeked out. "What are you—"

I didn't answer.

Sometimes there are no words.

And sometimes.

Sometimes you just might be surprised by the people in your life who don't need to hear any. Mace hesitated. For just a second. Then she opened the door a little wider. And let me in.

fifty-one

I opened my eyes.

I was in a soft bed. Curtains drawn at the window. I couldn't tell if it was day or night.

"I don't know...." Mace was talking quietly on the phone in the other room. I lay there, listening. "What do I—No... not like that. It's just...we get each other more now.... Okay. Do you want to talk to my dad again? No, that's fine. Okay. Bye, DiDi."

I heard her hang up with a soft click. And just like I knew she would, she didn't knock or bother me. She just let me be. Just like I needed. I guess maybe we did get each other.

I closed my eyes.

I was in one of the guest rooms in Mace's home. That's

where I was. In clean pajamas with little flowers all over them. I pulled the comforter up to my chin and let myself sink into the pillows and back into a place where I didn't have to think.

I opened my eyes.

It was morning and the pink water bottle was on the nightstand, along with a note: *Don't worry about school. We told them you're sick yesterday and today. Sandwich in the mini-fridge. Also, hydrate! M.*

That darn pink water bottle.

I smiled. And then I realized it was the first time I'd smiled since...

Since.

I reached out to pick up Mace's note—then drew my breath in and looked over to where I'd left my jeans. I slowly walked over and reached into the pocket. It was still there. A worn, folded KOB with nothing written on the front. The KOB that I'd promised to wait to read.

I broke the promise.

> *G—So if you kept your promise and waited to open this when I asked, we are on the hill right now and you are probably looking at me funny. Haha. Just kidding. Anyway, I'm going to tell you something I've never told anyone before, but I'm not going to write it. I'm going to say it out loud and you're the first person I want to say*

it to. Okay, so you can put this down now and look at
me. I'm ready. (And in case I forget to say it afterward,
thank you. I'm really, really glad you moved here.) T

I folded it, put it back into my jeans pocket, and crawled
back into bed.

Later that afternoon, I woke up partly because I was starving
and partly because I could hear Mace and her mom arguing
in the hall.

"—you run away and—"

"I told you why—you just didn't—"

"I'm putting my foot down. If I'm responsible, I say she
goes to school—"

"Mom, you're not even listening—"

"Just because you and your father—"

"Mom, stop! Stop it—"

I covered my ears and buried myself deeper in the blankets.

When Mace brought me dinner in the guest room, she set it on
the table and paused. Then left and came back with my backpack
and a small overnight bag. She sat down on the edge of the bed.
"My dad picked up some of your stuff from...anyway, he got
some of your stuff. I'm sorry. You have to go to school tomorrow."

fifty-two

Mrs. Tanglewood drove us to school the next day. I could tell she just didn't know what to say to the girl who had run away with her daughter. Who was staying in her guest room. Who hadn't stopped sleeping since she arrived.

I just sat in the backseat and watched as Mrs. Tanglewood sat as far left as she could in the driver's seat. And Mace sat as far right as she could in shotgun. Though I had a feeling Mrs. Tanglewood never called it shotgun.

When we got to school, I was lost. I didn't know what to do. I kept forgetting and wanting to follow the Recipe for Success again, but I wasn't that person anymore. I wasn't Galileo or Leia or G-Girl. I wasn't anyone.

And if I didn't know who I was, how was I supposed to know what Recipe to follow?

I sat in the front row in English, concentrating on Mr. McGuire the entire time. Pretending not to see Trip rushing out with his head turned away from me when class ended. I wasn't sure what to do when I saw Billy heading in my direction, but Mace was there. She leaned across the aisle casually, blocking him and asking about homework till I got away. I was so grateful, I forgot to be surprised.

At lunchtime, I tried to walk into the cafeteria with my chin up, but I turned back and ran. I hid in the girls' room for the rest of the hour and ended up not even eating lunch. But the gnawing in my stomach was nothing compared to the empty aching in my chest.

The next morning, I got the nerve to find Mr. McGuire in the teachers' lounge before class started and asked if I could use his classroom during lunch. I told him I needed the quiet time to catch up and that I'd eat my lunch and not make a mess. He didn't ask where I'd been or why I was behind. He just nodded and gave me a pat on the back.

I didn't have to worry about the cafeteria, because Mace had handed me a lunch that her mom had made. It was super-healthy-looking and pretty, too. A turkey sandwich with avocado and sprouts and some kind of yummy spread on bread with all these seeds in it. Wrapped in nice paper like it was from a sandwich shop. It was delicious. At least, the few bites I was able to force down were. I tried not to think about DiDi at home. Maybe making lunch for me and then remembering that I wasn't there. And Mace didn't say a word about me not going to the cafeteria. It's not like we really talked that much. We rode to school together with her mom, who had nothing to say, either. Mace and I looked at each other when we arrived. And then went our own way.

Mr. McGuire came into his classroom while I was staring and not eating. He nodded at me, then pulled out his own lunch and a bunch of papers and got to work at his desk. I tried not to look. To check and see if they were everyone's Truth poems. Mine was late. Before this week, I'd never handed in anything late in my life. I hadn't even started my poem. The truth was just too hard to think about.

Mr. McGuire came the next day, too. Not saying a word. Just nodding and going to work. I heard extra footsteps behind his and looked up to find Haven and Allie just kind of standing there in the doorway, looking nervous. Our eyes met and they both came rushing in.

They ran up to me and then stopped. Haven was biting

her lip and Allie was looking like if she had Banky just then, he'd probably be wrapped around her head three times and tied up in the biggest knot ever.

"Are you—are you okay?" Haven said. "I mean—we don't even know what hap—"

We all glanced at Mr. McGuire, but he had settled down at his desk, busy working.

"We care about you," said Allie. "Having you join Stargazers was the best thing that happened this year...."

"And it's not just Stargazers," said Haven. "It was...you know...hanging out...becoming friends."

Allie nodded and looked at me. "Anyway...we're having a meeting now. If you...?"

Haven nudged her. "You don't have to, but if you want. If you feel like it..."

I shook my head. Eyes full. Then pretended to go back to work. The Stargazers. I didn't belong. I wasn't named after a famous scientist, and the star on my forehead wasn't a sign proclaiming my great destiny. It was a mark that I was someone who had been pushed away.

I heard the girls shuffle over to Mr. McGuire. They started the meeting, talking in soft voices. I kept telling my feet to just get up and walk out, but I didn't know where to go. I couldn't stay in the girls' room for the rest of lunch, and I refused to go into the cafeteria. The nurse's office? Maybe. I had started to gather my things when I overheard part of the conversation.

"But why does it have to be now? Can't we just wait a couple of weeks, until...you know?" Haven's voice trailed off. I glanced up and saw her looking over at me.

"Not much we can do about it, ladies," Mr. McGuire said. "Sadly, meteor showers are just outside my powers of influence."

"Wait, I thought they were called shooting stars," Allie said. "*Meteor showers* sounds kind of like"—she made a face—"*meatier showers?* Ew."

"Okay," said Mr. McGuire. "Quick review. Shooting stars and meteors are the same things—bits of cosmic debris that leave the comet they came from to go on and form their own blazing path. It may seem like a random occurrence, but I think it a noble task."

I had stopped putting my things away and was listening to Mr. McGuire as hard as I could. "Think of it this way: In the end, whether you call them shooting stars or meteors, just like everything else in this universe, they have their time and their chance to show up—and, if they're lucky, a few people willing to witness their shining moment. And what more do you need than the right few people?" Mr. McGuire's voice grew soft. "So, my drifting bits of celestial debris, are you going to sputter out? Or grab your turn and blaze through the sky? That's the real question. And that's the truth"—I looked up and saw that even though he was talking to the girls, something about Mr. McGuire's kind smile seemed to be meant for me—"about shooting stars."

I got up and made my way over to his desk. I opened my mouth to say something. Maybe that I wanted back in.

Maybe that I missed my friends.

Maybe that I didn't want to lose my moment, either.

But before I could say any of those things, I was smothered by the four arms of Haven and Allie. And I realized I didn't have to say anything.

Pick Me Up

Now, I heard that in fancy restaurants, they serve you something like a dessert in the middle of the meal and they just call it a Refresher. It's supposed to cleanse your palate and make you forget everything you already ate so you can get all ready for the next course.

- 6 cups of fresh watermelon chunks, frozen
- 3 scoops of lemon sherbet
- 1½ cups water
- Juice from 1 lemon
- Mint leaves for garnish

Throw everything except the mint leaves in your blender and whip it up.

Pour into a 9-by-13-inch baking dish and freeze for an hour, or till it's nice and icy.

If you have a fancy glass, I think a scoop of this would be real pretty served in it. And you know what? Why don't you stick a little mint leaf on there, too!

Eat with a spoon.

Light, refreshing, and not too sweet. Just a little something to get you ready when you know there's still plenty more to come.

Serves 8–10.

fifty-three

riday, I took the bus back to Mace's house after school and went straight to the room where I was staying. It never occurred to me that Mace might be doing anything other than her zillion after-school activities as president of the Whatever-Whatever Club and then homework in her room, too. But it was Friday, and after days of being stuck in that guest room, I wanted to get out of there. Maybe walk around. I wondered if it would be weird to ask Mace to join me. We weren't friends, exactly, but we were ... something.

I tiptoed down the hall and listened hard. The house was quiet. Usually Mace left me alone till dinnertime and then brought food to my room. I wondered what she did the rest of the time. I hadn't really even seen the rest of the house.

No one seemed to be home.

I went down a quiet hall and turned a corner into the biggest whitest kitchen I'd ever seen. Mrs. Tanglewood was sitting all by herself at this gigantic table, just staring out the window. I made a quick move to back out, but the floor creaked. Dang. I guess there are creaky floors no matter where you go. When she saw me, she looked about as relaxed and comfortable as I felt.

"Oh...Leia," she said. "Won't you—did you want to come in?"

Now I began to back out for real. "No, that's okay. I didn't want to interrupt....I was just wondering where Mace was."

"You don't know?"

Know what?

I could only shake my head.

Mrs. Tanglewood got up and walked to the refrigerator. It had this big sliding glass door in front, so you could see everything inside. There were rows and rows of all-natural juices and bottled fizzy water and bowls filled with shiny apples and lemons and such. All standing there, perfectly lined up like soldiers. But then I noticed that if you looked really close, you could see in the back that it was kind of a mess. Tumbles of half loaves of bread and leftovers and stuff wrapped up in bumpy tinfoil.

"She's with your sister, DiDi. As she has been every afternoon this week."

"With D—" My voice came out a squeak. "With DiDi? Why? Doing what?"

"Why should I be informed? She and Mr. Tanglewood seem to have decided that they know better than I do about everything. Who am I?" Mrs. Tanglewood studied the glass front of the fridge. It looked perfect to me, but she grabbed a paper towel and gave it a wipe. "Why should I know anything? Where she runs away to...who she's with...why you're h—"

Mrs. Tanglewood turned her back to me and rubbed at that glass like it was a genie's bottle and she didn't know what to wish for. I knew what I'd wish. I'd want to know what was going on. What was Mace doing with DiDi? Probably talking about me. I'd thought somehow that Mace was on my side now. But she had always preferred DiDi. And here I was, finding out they had spent every afternoon for the last week together.

"I—I'm sorry," I said. "Do you want me to—Can I help you in here?"

Mrs. Tanglewood didn't turn around. "Oh, no thank you." She opened the fridge door and began to fiddle with the row of juices. Nudging them ever so slightly, till they completely hid the mess in the back. "I don't know why I bother. I might as well just give up. If it wants to be a mess, let it be a mess." She gave this sad little hiccup of a laugh and closed the door.

I looked at the glass door. It was like being in the fanciest grocery store ever. "Well, it—it looks perfect to me."

Mrs. Tanglewood sighed. She tilted her head to the side and then picked up the paper towel again and gave the fridge one last swipe. "It does, doesn't it?"

When Mace peeked in later, I was sitting at the little desk in the guest room, doing homework.

"Hi," she said.

"Hi," I answered, not looking up.

"Okay, so my mom said you found out how I'd been helping DiDi."

I don't know why I was surprised. One thing Mace has always been is direct. So now I was, too.

"Why? What are you doing? Why didn't you tell me?"

Mace came in and closed the door. She went over to the bed to sit down and paused before she began to talk again. "I don't know. . . . You've been really upset. DiDi has been really upset. Neither of you will tell me what happened, but it doesn't even matter. DiDi—DiDi is my friend and you . . . Well, anyway, she's had all these big plans and she needed help. Actually, Haven, Allie, Billy and Trip, and Mr. McGuire have been helping, too. I'm sorry, I—I asked them not to tell you yet. . . ."

Now I was completely confused. What big plans? What did they all have to do with anything?

Mace looked at me. "The Founder's Day Gala. Tomorrow. DiDi has been planning the menu since, like, the beginning of the year. She has all these great ideas. She just—well, she gets nervous about—about trying new things. . . . She's been there for me so much—I just wanted to do the same for her."

The Gala.

We'd said it was going to be our own personal birthday party. I'd promised DiDi I would help her. We even shook on it. But I never did.

"What have you been . . . how are you helping?"

"We've just been helping her with shopping and organizing and taste-testing and everything. . . ."

"But—your mom—"

Mace began to study her hands. "I tried to explain, but—my dad says she just needs time." She shook her head and then looked up. "You should come. I know she wants you to." Mace reached into her pocket and pulled out a KOB. "Here."

I took it and saw DiDi's strong clear writing on the outside. *Leia.*

I barely noticed Mace leaving as I slowly unfolded it.

> *Leia,*
>
> *I miss you more than I can say and I love you even more than that. I know you need your time and I know that this has been so hard for you, but I want to see you and I can't help that. You are the love of my life and the treasure of my heart and I am so proud*

of who you are and everything about you and I wish
I'd told you this every day since the beginning of time.
Will you please come to the Gala tomorrow? I'll be
there early setting up and I'll be waiting for you.
I love you more than the world.
DiDi

The words became a blur behind my tears. I'd never had a birthday in my life that didn't have me and DiDi in the kitchen together, making Twinkie Pie. In that second, I was feeling so many things. Confusion. Sadness. Longing. But mostly. Mostly. I missed DiDi. More than I could say. And I knew one thing at that moment. That if I belonged anywhere, it was at that Gala by her side.

fifty-four

There are different kinds of quiet.

There's the quiet you get after it rains and you watch the birds creeping out—looking to see if it's okay to start tweeting again. That's a good quiet. It makes you feel like anything is possible.

And then there's the quiet of Mrs. Tanglewood's car.

All week long, Mrs. Tanglewood had driven us to school with no music or conversation, her white-knuckled hands gripping that steering wheel in the ten and two o'clock positions. Mace sat in the front with her and I sat in the back. Each day, it was the same quiet drive. The kind of quiet you wish you knew how to break. But just can't figure out. The way to the Founder's Day Gala was no different.

I couldn't stop fidgeting in the backseat. Mace had lent me a pretty dress to wear with pink and green flowers all over it. I hoped her mother wouldn't mind. It wasn't a long drive to school, but with Mace and her mom in the car not talking, it felt like a million miles. I had heard them arguing again right before we left. It had sounded like a big one. Something about clones or lemmings or something. But I didn't catch it all.

When it was time to go, I could tell they weren't finished yet. I was just hoping they wouldn't decide to finish in the car.

At the first stop sign, Mrs. Tanglewood, still looking straight ahead, said in a low whisper, "How can you think that? I want you to be yourself."

"As long as myself is a clone of you, you mean," said Mace.

I shrank down as low as I could in the backseat.

"That's not true."

"Right. You don't hate my hair and my makeup."

Mrs. Tanglewood kept looking straight ahead. "I don't—hate it. I just—" Her voice cracked. She cleared her throat. "I just don't see why you need someone else—"

"Oh, right, because you and I have so much in common—"

"You know..." Mrs. Tanglewood lowered her voice. "For your information, I was a real rebel when I was your age."

"Right."

"I was."

"*You* were."

"Yes. One summer, your aunt Lily and I pierced each oth-

312

er's ears—with safety pins—right before we snuck out to see Joan Jett in the city. What do you think of that?"

The car behind us beeped.

Mrs. Tanglewood jumped in her seat. Then started driving again.

"That's—really? Was Grammy—did she ever find out?"

"Well, yes, of course, and she grounded us and made us take them out and wait till we were sixteen and got us classic pearl studs. I still have mine. I thought you could wear them when you—Or...we can get whatever you'd like...of course."

Mace didn't answer for a second. Then shrugged. "Whatever. I'll look at them. If you want."

"That would be fine."

"Fine."

"Fine...."

Mrs. Tanglewood continued driving toward the school. I eased up in my seat. The car got quiet again. But it was a little different this time. I leaned over just enough to peek into the space between them and saw that Mrs. Tanglewood's right hand had left its post at two o'clock and was resting on the middle console. Just a few inches from Mace's left.

fifty-five

As we pulled into the school parking lot, Mace nudged me and pointed out the window. Trip was standing across the way with a group of boys and girls.

"Wait," I said. "I'm sorry, Mrs. Tanglewood. Can I please get out here?"

"Oh, look. There's Trip. Do you want to get out here, too?" Mrs. Tanglewood pulled the car up to the sidewalk.

Mace looked at me. "No, Mom. Let's drop Leia here. Then we can park the car and—walk in together."

Mrs. Tanglewood paused. "That would be fine."

"Thank you, Mrs. Tanglewood. I'll see you inside." I slipped out of the car and began to walk toward Trip. Then stopped. He glanced up at me and back down at the ground again.

In the Recipe for Success, when you want to look confident, you take these firm straight steps and keep your chin up. Make eye contact and try and look like you know what's what. Which is kind of hard when the person you're trying to talk to turns and starts walking away as fast as they can in the opposite direction. To heck with the Recipe—I broke into a run.

"Trip!" I yelled, and I could hear my voice squeaking with everything I was feeling, and I'm guessing so could everyone else, but I didn't care. "Trip, please wait."

He stopped.

He didn't turn.

I ran up till I was right behind him. Then there was this big space of time where I couldn't speak and it didn't look like he could, either, even if he wanted to, and it was building and building, and as much as I wanted him to be the first to say something—how he missed me, how I was still his best friend, how everything was okay—I knew it wasn't. And I knew I had to be the first to speak.

I took a deep breath. "Trip." My voice cracked again and I cleared it. "I—I am so sorry." I shook my head and tried to start over. "When we first moved here, all I ever thought about was how I'd never really had . . . friends before. I'd never had a friend like you or Billy or Haven or Allie...or Mace." He looked up. "And with Mace, I was jealous and I...Trip, I just liked you. Really *liked* you liked you. Do you know what I mean? You are the best friend a person could have. You know every terrible thing about me and you stood by me and I paid you back by—" I started to cry for real. "And I'm so, so sorry I hurt you. You know I don't think any of those things I said—I just—I just want you to be you and I want us to be friends again. Please, please tell me you forgive me."

Trip looked at me a long time.

"G-Girl," he said, but I started crying even harder the second I heard that stupid nickname and realized how much I missed hearing it. "I'm sorry, too—"

"You? Saying sorry to me? For what?" I sobbed.

"For not going south—and for not knowing how you felt about, you know, about me. I just—I never ever would've guessed you liked me. Like that."

I laughed through my tears. "Because I always played it so cool?"

"No. Because of how much Billy likes you."

"Wha-huh?"

Now Trip laughed. "I thought you liked him back. You guys are always, you know, high-fiving each other and stuff."

At that very moment, Billy came bounding up to us, dribbling a basketball. He passed it to Trip and then turned to me and held up one hand. I looked at him in a daze and high-fived him.

"Hey, kids! G-Girl, where you been? Better get inside, it's going to start soon...." He held his hands out for the ball. Trip passed it back. "See ya." Billy grinned at me and ran off.

My mouth was open like a church door on Sunday morning. Trip reached out and hooked an arm through mine. "C'mon, let's go."

The Gala was in the Old Dining Hall, which is a funny name, I know. But Hill Prep is like two hundred billion years old, and back in the day, they used to have really formal meals served family style and everything. After they built the new cafeteria, the Old Dining Hall was only used for special occasions like school dances and holiday parties. It's a grand room for sure. The floors are dark and wide and there are big windows on each side. This giant oil painting hangs at one end by some famous artist who was a student here once.

At the other end, there's a big old grandfather clock that has been there since the beginning of time. I liked that clock. You could hear it tick a mile away. Though *Tick* wasn't really the right word for the kind of sound a big, fine clock like this made.

It was more like... *Tock*.

Tock... Tock... Tock.

All day long. Sure and steady.

Which makes sense to me, because that's how time passes when you're in the real world and not on some crazy TV cooking show. Sure and steady. And always moving forward.

My heart was pounding as I looked around for DiDi. I didn't see her anywhere.

But she was everywhere.

In the tables laid out all fresh and breezy with beautiful white cloths.

In the friendly flowers bending toward you at every turn.

And in the food.

The food.

Some things I recognized right away. Others I had to guess.

The cutest little appetizers with homemade potato chips, a golden bubbling cheese sauce, and swirls of roasted red peppers. It was like she'd taken the ingredients for EZ Cheeze sandwiches and pulled them apart, putting them back together in a totally new way. A way only DiDi could have thought of.

Secret Layered Salads were stacked into elegant little towers on a skewer with a sprig of something green and pretty on top.

Madder'n Heck Smashed Potatoes were there, only not all

that Mad anymore. Just golden and crispy-edged with some kind of creamy filling inside.

And rows of tiny teacups with a pastry leaf on top, baked like little mini–pot pies that had to be filled with Turn Over a New Leaf Turnover filling.

They were all there. Mama's recipes. Only for the first time...

For the first time, they were DiDi's.

Mrs. Tanglewood and Mace and Mrs. Davis were standing over a platter of little hors d'oeuvres. "These look so delicious," said Mrs. Davis.

"Well, I'm glad she decided to cater it," Mrs. Tanglewood said.

"I tried to tell you before, Mom. It's not catered," Mace said. "DiDi made it all, and a bunch of us helped."

I was happy for DiDi. I was. And I was so proud and so amazed by all her food, but I couldn't help the pit inside me that kept reminding me that this was supposed to be our Birthday Gala menu. That I'd promised her I would help and we would be partners, but instead I'd spent every weekend lying to her about being at the library while I was running off to do my own selfish thing.

Mrs. Davis looked around. "Is she here? Please tell her that it's all—it's all just lovely. Really." She smiled at me standing there with Trip.

Mrs. Tanglewood nodded. "It is. It really is."

"I—I'll tell her. I'll tell her when I see her."

"Hello, Leia. Hello, Trip."

We looked up. "Miss Homer?"

I guess I'd never seen her without one of those books of hers and dressed head to toe in mousy, mousy brown, but here she was in a flowy white dress with her hair all curled.

"You look—Why, you look just beautiful, Miss Homer," I said.

"You do," said Trip.

She blushed. "Thank you both—and thank you for all your help at the library. I don't know how we'd get along without you. Oh, I'd like to introduce you to my—my new friend." She beckoned to a man across the room.

It was like a slow-motion scene from a movie, the way he turned and walked toward us. His long hair flowing behind him. And truth is, it looked to me like the only loosening up he ever had to do was with that old ponytail.

"Hey, Kenneth," I said.

"Uh, h-hi, GiGi," he stammered. Then smiled shyly. And I have to say it was nice to know that changing your hair doesn't change who you are on the inside. Sometimes it just shows the world who you want to be.

"Have you seen my sis—" I stopped. Confused—and

anxious. DiDi had asked to me to come early, and here everything was already starting.

Trip glanced at me and stepped in. "Have you seen DiDi, Miss Homer?"

"She left," said Miss Homer.

"What?" I said.

"I was just coming over to tell you. She wanted me to pass on the message that she needed you to meet her back at your apartment."

I turned to Trip. "I have to go—I have to talk to her."

Trip nodded.

At that moment, his dad walked up and put an arm around him on one side and Mrs. Davis came over to his other side and did the same.

"Can we give you a ride?" she asked.

"No thank you," I said. "It's only a minute away and DiDi always—" I swallowed the tightness in my throat. "DiDi always says the best part of living in a Walking Town is walking."

I turned and hurried to the door.

Because even though I said it was a Walking Town.

I didn't walk.

I ran.

Everything else faded away. Trip. Miss Homer. The whole Gala. Everything.

Everything except for the steady sound of that grandfather

clock behind me, beating a sure and steady rhythm along with my heart.

Tock...Tock...Tock...

I ran out of the school that DiDi moved us 800 miles to get to.

Through the town where she worked day and night to give us the life we had.

Up those creaking stairs to the home where I had the one bedroom, while she slept on the sofa.

I ran, thinking of all my What Ifs.

Of everything that I had wished and hoped for in my whole life. And how if the host of that TV cooking show put a Mystery Basket in front of me, right then and there, if I had DiDi with me, I would be willing to face anything—even chicken feet and pancake mix.

Tock.

I opened the door.

DiDi's pretty curls swung free and loose as she looked up. The second our eyes met, I could feel my face running away from me, but this time—this time, I let it run to see where it would go, and it led me all the way into DiDi's arms and she was holding me and talking like we had never been apart.

"I wish I was smart like you, Double G. I wish I could say I had a recipe for everything that's happened in my life,

322

but I don't." She squeezed me harder. "Truth is, I was just a silly girl who thought she knew what was what. Snuck into some bar one night, looking for fun and lying about my age. Fell hard for some sweet-talking college boy out for a good time. I thought it was love, but when I—I got pregnant and he found out how old I really was, he took off. Lied to my face. I never heard from him again. Mama—she went crazy. She was drinking so much—she didn't care—she didn't want to hear about my silly broken heart. Figured I was out chasing every man in the county and—and accused me of stealing her low-life boyfriend next...." DiDi took a big ragged breath.

The tears were spilling out of me. "Oh, D—"

"She wasn't there for me, G—not for a second. But of all the things I didn't know, there was one thing I did: I wanted to be there for you. No matter what. I didn't want you wasting time being ashamed of who I was and what your history was like. I didn't want you stuck being Delta Dawn the Third. I just wanted...I wanted you to grow up believing you had the most amazing mama in the world—with the biggest dreams—and that you could be just like her...."

"I do, DiDi—I already believe it—and I already know it. I think you're the brains in the family," I said into her shirt. "If I could be anything like you, I'd wish for anything more."

"Dang it, where is a darn tissue when you need one—don't

you dare wipe your nose on your sleeve, girl!" And we laughed and DiDi pulled some paper napkins out of somewhere and wiped my face.

"I was at the Gala, D. I saw what you did—everything—everything was beautiful and—and I'm so sorry I didn't help you. I know I promised, and I wish I had been there—"

"Shhh." DiDi tucked the hair away from my face. "I told you we'd do it right this time, didn't I? And none of it ever would've happened without all your yakking and bothersome suggestions all this time."

"Hold on, I'm the yakky one?"

DiDi laughed. "Come here, G. I have something I want to show you."

I looked over to where she was leading me.

A beautiful cut-glass punch bowl stood on the counter. I looked back at DiDi and she nodded. I stepped closer.

Through the sparkling glass, I could see beautiful layers of red fruit and golden cake.

Topped with a snowy-white blanket of whipped cream.

"D?"

She held out a brown paper bag. "I got them at the Super Saver. I wanted to wait till you were here. I just…I couldn't make it without you, G…."

And she tipped the bag onto the counter, sending a jumble of ruby-red fruit bouncing across the top, rolling every which way. Some off the counter and some to the floor and some right into my outstretched hands.

I whipped back around to face her.

"Well, it *is* supposed to be our own personal Birthday Gala," she said, and through the tears that were starting again, I could hear a famous DiDi babble coming on. "There isn't pudding or bananas or Nilla wafers, so we can't really call it Twinkie Pie anymore, but then Mr. McGuire was talking about your class and how poetry was a way to take things from your past and—and make them into something beautiful—on your own terms—and I thought, well, if it was okay with you—maybe we could give it a new name—"

And then I was laughing and she was laughing or maybe we were both crying, but it didn't matter, because I could feel the words rising up in the air, lighter than anything, as we said them together:

"Cherries in the Snow."

I threw my arms around her. "Get out."

She held me close. "If you let me back in. Happy birthday, Double G."

I pulled back so I could look her straight in the eyes. "Happy birthday, Double D." And I said it loud and I said it proud, because if we were going to be darn bra sizes, at least we were the biggest ones there.

And truth is, at that moment, I didn't know exactly

who I was or who DiDi was, and mostly, I realized I didn't have to. Life had handed us one heck of a Basket of Mystery Ingredients, and we were just going to have to figure out what we wanted to do with them. Keep some things, change others, and the recipe—well, we'd just make it up as we went along, and whatever we ended up with, the most important thing was, we would make it together.

Cherries in the Snow

This is our version of Cherries in the Snow, but DiDi and I think you should make your own.

You'll need two 3-ounce packages of soft ladyfingers—though if you want to use pound cake or your own cake, I say why not?

Whipped Topping Layer

You can buy your favorite whipped topping at the store or make it yourself.

- 2 cups heavy cream
- 1 teaspoon vanilla
- 2 tablespoons confectioners sugar

Beat the cream until it just starts to make peaks, then whip in the vanilla and sugar.

Like anything else in life, for heaven's sake, don't overwhip it. Cover it and put it in the fridge.

Cherries Layer

Now, I will not make a fuss if you want to use cherry pie filling, but we decided to make up our own version with fresh cherries, so give it a try, please.

- 2 cups fresh cherries, halved and pitted, keeping aside a handful of whole cherries for the top
- 2 cups fresh cranberries
- ½ cup sugar
- 1 cup water
- 3 navel oranges

Put your halved cherries, cranberries, sugar, and water in a saucepan, and bring to a gentle boil. Stirring, cook for 15 minutes till it's nice and thickened. Let cool. Place a wire mesh strainer over a mixing bowl and carefully pour the sauce into the strainer. Work the sauce through the strainer with the back of a wooden spoon. You will have 2 cups of smooth, creamy cherry sauce. With a sharp knife, supreme your oranges. This means cut both ends off deep enough to reach the fruit. Then carefully cut all the peel off, leaving perfectly bald, juicy oranges. Now very carefully cut out each little orange section by going in one side of the membrane and out the other, leaving the lining behind.

You'll be left with three pulpy orange pinwheels. Squeeze all the juice out of them into a bowl and set this aside. Take all your orange sections and add them to the cherry sauce. Then cover and put in the fridge.

When you're ready to assemble your Cherries in the Snow, get out your prettiest glass trifle bowl. Though come to think of it, this would also look pretty served in big fancy parfait glasses. You know the ones that look like you bought them at the Giant Supply Store? Either way, the choice is up to you.

Anyway, start with a layer of ladyfingers. Drizzle with your saved fresh orange juice. Spoon a layer of cherry-orange sauce. Then whipped cream.

Repeat until you end up with the whipped cream.

Scatter some pretty cherries on the top.

epilogue

Dear Mr. McGuire,
I know this is late and I'm sorry.
On the following page, please find my Truth Poem.

The Truth About Twinkie Pie

The Truth About Twinkie Pie
is that making it
is kind of like making a Life.
Because it doesn't matter
if what you put in it
is exactly what you figured and planned
as long as it's what you hope and dream
so when everything comes together
you know you're making something
so amazing
and delicious
and completely yours
that all you want to do
is hold it way up high
and shout out with all your might
"Look out, world! Sweet Stuff coming through!"

—and I'm not talkin' about the Twinkie Pie.

P.S. Also attached is a report on the relationship between poetry and science. I hope you will consider this as extra credit in order to bring my grade back to an A+.

P.P.S. DiDi wants to have all the Stargazers over Saturday for dinner again, but you don't have to call them. I'll just text everyone. No big deal. See you then!

P.P.P.S. Oh, I meant to tell you, the week after the meteor shower (so cool!), I went and read that book you lent me on my namesake, Mr. You Know Who. Did you know that when he was first trying to figure out what he wanted to be, he heard about telescopes but didn't know how to get one? I mean, it's not like there were any 24-hour telescope stores around. So you know what he did? He figured out how to make his own. I think that just might be my favorite thing about him so far.

Sincerely,
Your student and fellow Stargazer,
Galileo Galilei Barnes

RECIPE FOR HOW TO FOLD A KOB

Take one sheet of 8½-by-11-inch paper. Try not to use the kind that rips out of notebooks and leaves all those weird little flappy things up the side. Though you could always trim them off.

Write your message.

Fold the paper in half the long way, keeping the message on the inside. Then fold that in half the long way again. You should have a long, skinny strip of paper.

Put the paper on a table in front of you up and down like the number 1.

This part is a little tricky:

Put your left hand on the top half of the 1.

Take the bottom with your right hand and fold it over to the right at an angle, so that the paper looks like a capital letter *L*—but with a triangle cut out of the left corner. Try to get both sides of the *L* exactly the same length. Smooth it down firmly.

Now take the bottom of the *L* and fold it under itself so it comes out the left side and you have a backward *L* with a little triangle folded into the corner. Smooth the edge down.

Take the top of the *L* and fold it behind itself so you have a backward, upside-down *L* with a triangle showing in the upper corner. Smooth the edge down.

Take the bottom and tuck it into the triangle pocket. Smooth it.

And take the left side and tuck it into the triangle pocket over that. Smooth all the corners down.

Flip it over and write the name of the person you are giving it to... or directions like *Read Now!*

Or *Read Later.*

Or you can always leave it blank. It's up to you.

Have fun.

author's note

A note about the recipes in this book:

Anytime you decide to cook, please do me a favor and start with clean hands. I'm serious. Go now. Wash your hands with soap and hot water. Sing "Happy Birthday" in its entirety during the soaping. And sing the whole thing again for the rinsing. It's what my brother Max does, and he's an awesome cook and never gets sick.

Please make sure that you are supervised by an adult in all cooking activities. Learn the proper way to handle knives and to work around a hot stove.

Some of the recipes in this book include uncooked items. Be aware that there is always risk associated with the consumption of these things.

Be aware of food allergies. Replace any allergens with ingredients that you and your parents know are safe for you.

And lastly, this is what I think. Be happy. Eat well. And try to do everything in moderation. For the sake of the very specific personality of one character, Mama, in this story, ingredient choices were made according to her history and preferences. Please feel free to replace high-fat ingredients with lower-fat ones. Sometimes you might need to buy fresh cherries in the middle of winter, but do try to shop locally when you can. Learn about what is best for your body, and make healthy choices on a daily basis. But also, I think that sometimes you have to have real butter.

Play with these recipes. Have fun. Make them your own. It's your Basket of Ingredients. What you do with it is up to you.

Enjoy!

P.S. The amount of maraschino cherries it would take to make whipped cream the actual color of Cherries in the Snow lipstick is terrifying. I know this from experience. So I will ask for a little leeway with this bit of fiction.

acknowledgments

I wish I could think of the perfect introduction to this section. Something that would encompass the vast and impossible range of emotions I am feeling right now, but I think I will have to settle for simply saying

THANK YOU!

Two people believed in this story very early on:

My agent, Sarah Davies, who made clear from the very beginning her passion and determination to fight for this story (and me).

My editor, Alvina Ling, who first saw this story at an NJSCBWI conference critique in 2011. Thank you for your guidance and patience and, most of all, for trusting me to do what needed to be done.

To Kathy Temean, who was the RA of NJSCBWI in 2011 and made the decision to place me with Alvina on a hunch that it would be a good match. (Trust me, writers, go join SCBWI!)

To all the amazing people at Little, Brown Books for Young Readers, especially Bethany Strout, Christine Ma, Sasha Illingworth, Nikki Garcia, Barbara Perris, Faye Bi, Jenny Choy, Victoria Stapleton, Melanie Chang, Andrew Smith, and Megan Tingley.

To the tribe known as SCBWI—especially Lin Oliver, Steve Mooser, Kim Turrisi, and Sarah Rutenberg—as well as their entire team of magic-makers without whom this manuscript (and others to follow) would never have made it out into the world. (Did I mention to join SCBWI yet?)

To the NANOWRIMO community, without whom I would never have finished that very first rough draft.

Sometimes you just know within seconds of meeting someone that they will be your kid-lit soul mates for life. To Joyce Wan, Dianne De Las Casas, Marcie Colleen, Amber Alvarez, and Betsy Devaney for laughs and support and steadfast friendship in the wake of neuroses. And to Sarah Aronson for a life-changing favor to a stranger.

A heartfelt thank-you to those who went out of their way to spend time with me and talk of things simply out of the kindness of their hearts and souls. Susan Edwards-Bourdrez for helping me to remember some of the magical details of middle school. Dan Green for bringing the shooting stars a little closer for this novice Stargazer. Hunter Breckinridge Davis for the loan of two-thirds of the best name of the nicest boy ever. Josh First for the much-needed ammo tutorials. Elyse Rose-Coster for her culinary expertise. Linda Roberts Mueller for sharing her story. And especially Behzod Sirjani for sharing his and inspiring a new element in mine. (I'll say it again: Everyone should be so lucky to have the kind of friend that Ryan had in you.)

To my dear friends Keith, Amanda, and Corbin "The Cub" Cartagine for their southern hospitality and love.

To my formerly southern brother, Max—you only get partial credit for "Hot Stuff! Coming Through!" but full credit for your help and support, particularly for introducing me to Terry Miller and Amy Gutzmer, who were so generous with answering questions and sharing their knowledge and time.

To Stine and Mom: This is a story about sisters and mothers—I have been blessed in both. Mom—for making home-cooked meals every single day for as long as I can remember and letting me loose in the kitchen when I wanted. And Stine—this journey all began with a punchbowl cake and some pretty impressive Jell-O molds at your bridal shower. I love you.

In memory of my father, whose first home in the US was teaching in Auburn, Alabama, where he forever reminisced over how popular and beloved he was in the South from the first day he set foot on southern soil, because (as he explained to us) who else could claim that everywhere they went in Alabama they were called Honey and Sweetheart? Only you, Dad. xoxo Miss you.

Most of all to my family:

Peter—for talking me down from many a tree, for your love and support and steadfast belief from the beginning.

Jasmine—my first reader and editor. I'm really sorry I forgot to put an ad in the yearbook for your graduation...but I was busy making you this.

And Tiger, my future storyteller—your kind heart and spirit and creativity (and your twisted humor) amaze me daily.

You are the loves of my life.

P.S. Revlon's Cherries in the Snow Super Lustrous lipstick is NOT discontinued. It can be found online and in stores that carry Revlon products.

P.P.S. (Oh, but I do wish they would bring back that fabulous gold case.)

FEB 0 4 2015

GLENCOE PUBLIC LIBRARY

3 1121 00395 0687

WITHDRAWN

RENEW ONLINE AT
http://www.glencoepubliclibrary.org
select "My Library Account"
OR CALL 847-835-5056

DATE DUE

MAR 1 4 2015	
MAY – 4 2015	
WNK	
SEP 2 3 2015	
DEC 2 3 2015	
JAN 0 4 2016	
JUN 3 0 2016	
APR 2 2 2018	

PRINTED IN U.S.A.